CHANGE

The Numismatic Odyssey of a 1963D Quarter (With Commentary)
By

Michael K. White

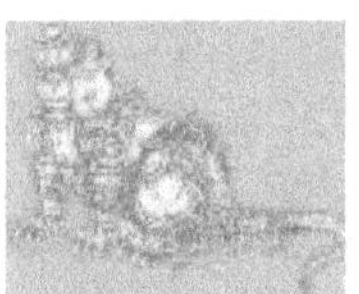

BGI BOOKS
New York-Paris-Marble Arch-Greeley-Johnstown-Arlington
October 5, 2004-September 5, 2012
With Thanks to Dianna Stark, Brian Greene, Matt Lubich, and Kyle Hogg

"A Single Flame Can Light Ten Thousand Fires."

-The Teachings of Buddha

"The process by which the Mint makes coins has advanced greatly since 1792. The first Philadelphia Mint used harnessed horses to drive the crude machinery that produced our coinage. The manual process required heating of metals in a blacksmith-like furnace, and flattening them into sheets by repeated trips through rollers. Coin shapes were then punched out of the metal sheets, and these were hand-fed into machines that stamped on coin faces. The coin making process was a physical and tedious one and imperfect coins were frequent.

Today, the Philadelphia and Denver Mints—which employ a highly-automated version of the same based steps used in 1792—often produce millions of coins for circulation in 24 hours. The modern Philadelphia and Denver facilities together in recent years have produced as many as 28 billion coins in a single year."

-Official United states Mint Website

Summer 2063
<u>Thule County, OKLAHOMA</u>

There are black clouds in the sky.

Ominous and majestic cumulonimbus clouds owned by huge moisture syndicates hover forebodingly over the late summer Oklahoma plains. The Arkansas Tampax Trojan River is running fast, green and stinking, teeming full of thrashing northern snakehead fish, riding the river west, devouring everything in their path.

When the river is running, they seldom come upon shore. Lately however, and in ever increasing numbers, they have been coming onto shore much more often in the past five years.
It is dusk.

The air hangs heavy with fetid humidity as a herd of snuffling snakeheads leave the river, dragging their big bellies across the hard scratchy ground. Voraciously, they consume everything in their path, garbage, plants, cans, dogs, anything at all. The largest of them, at over four feet in length, is on point, like a general, twisting its black blinkless eyes back and forth in search for food. The hungry herd of Frankenfish continues forward, snorting, gasping and eating, fulfilling a destiny so ancient it hardly seems real at all.

 The sky breaks open and the rain starts to come.

The snakehead fish can breathe easier now and their skin is smoothed and soothed by the return of their element. Lighting strobes the sky filling the air with ozone, Thunder rumbles as the thick heavy patented clouds collide.

As the herd of fish move forward, a glint of something in a small perfectly shaped black disk catches the largest fish's attention in the mud and reflexively the mighty fish uses its massive tooth lined lower jaw to scoop at the ground, clawing up and swallowing the smoothly worn and tarnished black wafer without a second thought.

It is an old coin, a 1963D Quarter dollar, one of 135,288,184 minted that year.

May 1890
<u>Rifle, COLORADO</u>

Only pressure can change one thing into another.

In terms of time, these transformations can seem endless, but that's because time is just something, we all agree on rather than something that is real.

It's not the time it takes but the change it makes.

In geological terms it takes billions of years to make a piece of silver ore. The processes involved leave their scars etched on the silver crystal's facets in a language that we are too uneducated to read completely. It was formed deep in the earth by compression and pressure, heat and cold, expansion and contraction, fire and water, and as a piece of silver ore, it rested nestled and senseless in a timeless journey of eons like a tiny seed inside a very large piece of fruit.

There are many pieces of silver ore on planet earth, a tiny fraction of which have already been discovered and transformed, but many more still lay waiting for the day of their initiation into whatever it is they will become. They are not sentient by any means, at least as far as we understand what sentience actually is, but merely mute observers, bearing witness and speaking only to one another in the secret and ancient language of rocks.

The piece of silver ore that would eventually become a 1963D Quarter saw its first rays of sunlight on May 5, 1890 just outside of Cripple Creek, Colorado. It emerged from a shovel full of black mountain dirt dug up by Richard Ostendorf, a novice gold miner from Bug Bay, Ohio.

Richard had been west only a few months, having come by train from St. Louis to make his fortune. Back home in Ohio was a girl waiting for him to return, Missy Snead, a plump crack toothed prairie flower who unbeknownst to Richard had died miserably from a typhoid contagion only weeks after he left for the West.

Richard had never spent springtime in the mountains and his heart was filled with the sights sounds and smells of what was all around him. He was still a relatively young man at 31, but he had been through much. His father had died from a miniball in the face at Cold Harbor, just weeks before the end of the war. Richard had hated his father, who beat him, and was not sorry to know he had been killed.

A bird sang and Richard stopped digging, listening to the unfamiliar melodious call of a bird he had never heard before. A distant *Tatatatatatat* from a woodpecker with a sharp ivory colored beak echoed in answer and a small fragrant gust of wind made the budding trees rustle like a giant woman's dress. It blew a delicious brew of scents; pine and dirt and weeds and distant rain. Richard thought of Missy and he stopped digging, lost in the moment where his past and present merged. He smelled in his memory the stale ancient Ohio smells of coal oil and tobacco and sweat and bread baking and fireplace smoke and hay and hemp and horses and Missy, all dim and manufactured next to the fresh easy gusts that pulsed through the high Colorado sky.

He felt his face, the stubble and heavy lines that creased. He had caught sight of himself in a store window last month in Colorado Springs and had been shocked. His hair was turning, what was left of it. His face had become longer, his eyes duller. He looked away from such a mirage and retreated to the mirror in his mind, where he was as he had once been, a strong young man with a full head of thick dark hair, eyes shining like silver coins with dreams of glory right behind them.

It made Richard sad now to think that there would be nothing left of him when he died. Assuming he would have children with Missy and they would go on to do great things, he himself had done nothing but scratch out a living hemp farming in Ohio until his mother finally died and he was free to go west and make his fortune. He never thought he would take to the mountains so. Their majesty and beauty made him reconsider his lack of belief in God. Sometimes when the wind gusted, he could hear God's voice, whispering to him. The words were like the ends of dreams; powerful and unattainable, just on the edge of comprehension.

Richard looked at the ground where he was digging. There were rocks and stones everywhere. He never knew there could be so many different kinds of rocks in the world and here in just one little place there seemed to be so many he could hardly understand it. They were like stars in the sky or drops of water in the ocean. There were just so many that he could see and he knew there was many more right below the surface. Most of them were valueless to him but some held the ability to change a man's life. He couldn't fathom how all these rocks came to be created. Did God craft each and every one? And no two were alike. Just like snowflakes and presidents.

A glint caught Richard's eye.

The bird called again; this time closer.

Tatatatatatat. The white billed-woodpecker answered from farther away.

Another gust of wind. He thought he smelled a fire.

 Richard bent over and dug up a little rock about the size and shape of a baby chick's head. It was surrounded in the ground by small thin, white rocks that looked for all the world like a rib cage. Richard rolled the rock over in his hand. The telltale crystals sparkled in the mid-morning sun and Richard's heart started beating hard. Everything suddenly seemed sharper to him up high in the mountains and when his heart beat like this and the surge went through him, he could almost believe everything would turn out the way he hoped for so long. Now everything would finally change. He rolled the heavy little rock around in his hand.

He knelt close and poured some creek water from his jug over it to clean it. The water felt cool and good. It was the first time in many centuries that the rock had felt the cool embrace of water. It began to radiate and shine in his hand and he could see from all the dull rocks around him that it was special. It reflected light back to him in such a way as to seem to glow from within.

He looked closely at the ground for more. Nothing glinted, but Richard noticed that the surrounding rocks were in a sort of pattern. They were unnaturally white and somehow familiarly shaped. He picked one up and examined it closely. It looked like a bone, but it couldn't be because it was a rock. There were more, tiny little white rocks that for all the world looked just like bones.
 Then he found a skull, a skull made from rock. It looked like a fish with sharp jagged teeth and he could even make out the tail, but he knew it was impossible. Because there were what looked like little legs too. His mind was on the verge of grasping something, of understanding something he didn't really want to understand. He kicked at the white bone shaped rocks and scattered them. He was seeing things. It was because he was up so high in the mountains after all those years in Ohio. His mind wandered with the breeze. He thought about it all and about nothing.

Springtime perfume from the wind.

A bird singing in a voice he was hearing for the first time.

Tatatatatatat. A faint and far away answer.

A woman's dress rustling.

Just the hint of a distant fire.

In his hand, silver.

May 1890-November 1963

For many years the silver rock would remain in its native state, along with other chunks of silver that silently suffered with incessant vanity about the toxic proximity to air and water and the eroding effect it had on their glittering shine.

In 1918, during the First World War all the silver hunks from that region of the Colorado Rockies were melted down, smelted and refined until they were formed into identical small smooth shiny ingots which were carefully stacked cross wise with layers of excelsior between them and shipped in special wooden boxes to the mint in Denver.

For decades the ingots would lie atop each other in the dark gloomy storage vault. Sometimes there were bats. They squeaked and flew crazily around the vaults. Their droppings tarnished many of the ingots. The decades rolled by, much like they did underground. The vaults were alive with spiders, who constructed entire civilizations and waged organized war against the sugar ants. The sugar ants built monuments to their God and fought the spiders in epic battles all mutely observed by the ingots. There was sometimes light, but mostly it was dark.

It wasn't until the tense and clattering year of 1962 that the mint's Master of the Ingots, Leon Lesage finally got to the pallet of silver bars which contained the silver made from the rock found by Richard Ostendorf in 1890. From this ingot fifty quarters were struck at the federal mint in Denver on a snowy December day just before Christmas. The lot of coins that contained our special Quarter was included in a shipment to Dallas, Texas where it was distributed to a local bank and in turn given in change to a local business, where it entered circulation. For the first six weeks of its existence, the Quarter sat in downtown Dallas in a white sackcloth bag with hundreds of others just like it.

The Quarter turned up in Fort Worth at the end of February, when it was used by Thomas Lyman to buy a pack of Lucky Strike cigarettes at a corner grocery.

The Quarter was given in change later that day to Ross Mcpheeters, a music teacher at Huey P. Long Junior High in Lexington, Louisiana, He kept the Quarter in his pants pocket for several days until he used it to buy gasoline for his new dirt colored Plymouth Valiant.

The Quarter was given in change to Mary Kinke a teenage girl who was purchasing some Kotex pads for the very first time. Her blushing embarrassment was noted by the leering drug store clerk Marc Hillk, a fifty-year-old father of nine. Mary kept the Quarter in a thin china cup that was her great grandmother's back in the Old Country. Her great grandmother had brought it to America with her when she came over on the sister ship of the Titanic in 1913. The cup was so thin and fragile that you could see light through it. Mary had the Quarter with her when she took a trip to Nashville with her family. She spent it at a Laundromat, surreptitiously washing her aunt's sheets after her cousin Ricky took her virginity one summer night after church camp.

The Quarter was rolled by the owner of the Nashville Laundromat and picked up with other quarter rolls by a Brinks truck. It was then taken to The First National Bank of Little Rock Arkansas, where it was distributed to a Skaggs Drug Store. It was then given in change to Schyler Petersen, a lonely teenage boy who quickly spent it on a plate of French fries at Bow-O-Mat.

The Quarter was given in change at Bow-O-Mat to Henry Galoute, a ball shine machine salesman out of Oklahoma City. He took the

Quarter home with him, where his wife fished it out of his pants pocket and put it in a peanut butter jar full of other coins.

The Quarter remained in the peanut butter jar until early October, when Iris Galoute lost it in a friendly poker game with her mom Gina and her sister-in-law Betty. Betty used the quarter to buy some bottles of pop for her kids, Jacky, Tracy and Bridget. The Quarter was again rolled and processed at the First National Bank of Dallas Texas where it was given in change to Jack Ruby, a nightclub owner who then used it to buy dog food for his two dachshunds. It was then given in change the first week of November to Mrs. Ruth Paine at the Piggly Wiggly store in Irving Texas.

November 1963
<u>Dallas, TEXAS</u>

Lee coolly walked away from the eruption and quickly down the stairs. He was outwardly calm but his heart was pounding and his mind was racing, clear and sure. He hurried without hurrying, taking two steps at a time, not like a desperate man but like a boy anxious to be somewhere else. His mouth was dry and he was glad he had the foresight to stop the pop machine man earlier in the day and ask for change.

Lee pushed open the door to the employee lounge. He was not breathing heavily. He pulled a Quarter he had swiped from a candy dish that morning from his pants pocket and slipped it into the pop machine. A cold Dr. Pepper rumbled out and Lee popped the cap off the bottle on the front of the machine and took a cool sweet foaming gulp from the cold green glass bottle.

His change clinked into the slot but before he could even swallow the fizzy drink a red-faced, nearly hysterical policeman in a white motorcycle helmet was pointing a pistol at him, screaming at him to put up his hands. Lee complied as he was swallowing the bubbly soda.

"Does this man work here?" The policeman shouted at Mr. Truly, Lee's boss who was huffing and puffing behind. A faint roar of excitement was drifting up from the lower level like smoke.

"Yes, yes he does," Mr. Truly wheezed and the policeman darted away, taking the stairs two at a time, with Mr. Truly staggering behind him, a cigarette dangling from his lips.

Lee put his hands down and took another drink of the Dr. Pepper. It wasn't a huge drink, even though he could have easily drained the bottle in one gulp. He figured there wouldn't be any more work today and besides, he had to get going. He collected his change from the pop machine and made his way quickly downstairs out into the bright and unseasonably warm sunlight.

December 1963
Austin, TEXAS

Orlando Bernal hated church. He had always hated it, but as a younger boy he hated it because it was boring and stole his play time from him while threatening him with hot eternal flaming hell. Now as a fifteen-year-old he saw all of the hypocrisy inherent in it and he felt he needed to stay away. This was easier said than done. His mother wouldn't allow him to skip church, not even when he was sick,

"That's when you need it the most mijo." She had said, making him get up out of a warm bed and get dressed. As he sat fuming at the table while she tried to get him to eat something before, they left, he stared straight ahead and thought about the stainless-steel Ingersoll pocket watch he had seen at Woolworth's the day before. It was a shiny watch that he immediately coveted. It came with a nice chain and clip so he could hook it to the back of his jeans. It was a watch that said something about a man. All his friends wore wristwatches with twistoflex bands, but Orlando felt different.

He watched his mother cut up an apple. first in half and then into fourths, for no good reason at all. He watched her as she scooped up the little cubes of apple and tossed them out the back door for the squirrels.

"What time is it Mom?" he asked her.

"Oh, I don't know mijo." She sighed.

He had scrounged up the five dollars that the watch cost, but he could find nothing else for the tax that he knew would be added on. Things always cost more than advertised. Then his mother had given him a Quarter for the collection plate. It was a new Quarter, still shiny and bright and he knew it would be just enough for the tax his stainless-steel Ingersoll pocket watch. wasn't this a message from God saying it was okay to get the watch? It was the exact amount he needed and there it was, in his hand.

So now the organ music was playing and the Pastor, a man named Oaten whose complexion matched his name, had just gotten done haranguing the assembled, red faced yelling at them about what bad people they were. Then he asked for money. Orlando saw the kind of car he drove. He clutched the Quarter tightly in his hand. He wasn't keeping this money from God but from this pasty little man who hated him and everyone else who was sitting and listening to him.

Orlando figured that he and God would work everything out someday. That if God was God, he would understand how a man needed a good sturdy stainless steel pocket watch. How he didn't feel like a bad person and how if God really cared about the things Pastor Oaten had screamed about then Orlando did not want to believe in that kind of God.

The basket came to his row. It overflowed with money. Orlando thought that his measly Quarter wasn't going to make that big of a difference to the Pastor, with his gold rings are the jeweled cross he wore around his neck. Orlando's Quarter wouldn't even shine his shoes. But it would change Orlando's life if he kept it for himself.

And then the basket was nestled in his lap and Orlando felt the eyes of the entire congregation upon him. Of course, they weren't.

He looked at the money in the basket and he longed to take it all, to take it and run with it, but ashamed, he dropped his Quarter into the basket and wouldn't ask his mother what time it was.

February 1964
New York, New York

The winter drizzle left the streets shiny like in movies and this night Manhattan looked like it should look, vibrant, clean and sparkling. It was evening, just after dusk and outside the Ed Sullivan Theatre on Broadway a crowd restlessly churned like wheat on a windy day.

"Are they already in there? Did you see them drive in? Are they there in this building? Just these walls away?" A tiny girl beseeched Myra Centingal, her face twisted and desperate. Myra had no answer. She had heard from some other girls that a black Cadillac limousine had indeed pulled into the service entrance behind the alley of the theatre but she didn't want to say anything. This was her first trip alone into the city from Queens, where she lived in a brownstone walk up with her parents.

Myra had told her parents that she was going to her friend Joyce Johnson's house to study for a history test. It was about the Jamestown colony and the early days of the settlement there. She told her mother that she and Joyce were doing a presentation on the Lost Colony of Roanoke. She had lied.

Myra was not used to lying to her parents. Indeed, this was the very first time, but she couldn't help it. She knew they would not allow her to come into New York on a Sunday night. They didn't understand. They could never understand. They did not know that everything was different now.

Everything.

When her mother first heard the music on the radio, she had tisked and right away she had started to criticize it. "If they're so English how come they sing in American accents?" She had accused. Myra's father had said even less. He didn't care about music at all. It was all just noise to him. He only knew two songs. One was "The Ballad of Ira Hays" and the other was not. The only record album he owned was a solemn record of Douglas MacArthur's farewell speech to Congress which always made her giggle because it was so corny.

Myra had collected her babysitting money, fifteen dollars and some change, and rode the subway into the city. She felt like Dorothy coming into Oz. She had never done anything like this before. She didn't even have a ticket to the show. Just being there was enough. She understood what the tiny girl had meant when she had said, "Just these walls away?" Myra felt that she was a part of something important.

The police were putting up barricades around the theatre now. Several of them were astride horses that clip clopped on the hard pavement of Broadway. The crowd had grown bigger and the drizzle seemed to vanish in a haze until the evening turned cold crisp and sharp. Myra clutched a Quarter in her hand, just in case she needed it to call home. She had run out of nickels after treating herself to a dinner at the Automat. There you put nickels into slots and slid open a tiny glass door that held whatever it was you wanted to eat, from roast beef with gravy to apple cake. She had gotten a cheese sandwich and tomato soup but she hardly ate at all. She was way too excited. It was like a dream.

In the past month she had collected every picture of them she could. Her mother disapproved, but Myra didn't care anymore. She didn't care about anything except the Beatles. They had become her whole life and it seemed like it happened over night. She knew that at fourteen she was way too old to be crushing on singers, but

she couldn't help it. They were complete strangers in every way but a deep throb inside told her that she knew them.
When she had first heard them on the radio ("That boy/ took my love away...") it spoke to something deep inside of her. Not necessarily a feeling as much as an urge. An urge to scream.

"Here ya trowe dese at 'em. Dey like it in Engal land." A fat girl with braces and pimples thrust a handful of warm slimy jelly beans into Myra's hand and moved off through the crowd repeating the mantra to every girl in her path. "Dey like it in Engal land..." Myra opened her hand and looked at the jelly beans, sodden from sweat, sticky and fragrant and leaving brightly colored stains on the inside of her palm smearing the shiny Quarter she clutched.

Suddenly a man was standing before her with thick black glasses. He was frowning down at her. "You." he said as a quickening, cascading twirl of girls started to surround him like a funnel cloud. "You. You. Over there. You and you." He said to a few other girls who were stamping and pawing the pavement with their feet. He jerked his head to the side indicating that the chosen should follow him and they did, the rest of the girls wailing and protesting, boiling and churning.

Myra and the others mutely followed the man right into the front of the Ed Sullivan Theatre. The woman at the box office nodded to the man and allowed them to pass amid the buzzing furious crowd of older people in suits and dresses, smoking and coughing and chit chatting like it was any other regular day. Myra was annoyed. Didn't they know?

One of the girls was talking, asking the man a million questions in a strained voice but he kept walking as if not hearing her. He led them into the auditorium itself, surprisingly smaller than it seemed on TV. Myra could see the stage with its closed curtain and the two huge cameras mounted on wheeled dollies. She saw the monitors

that ringed the stage and just as it hit her where she was, she realized that the man had led them to the front row.
"Stay here if you know what's good for you." He said in a cloud of ash and cigarette smoke that smelled like her grandma's bedroom. They obeyed, because they knew what was happening. She could feel it behind her breastbone and in the pit of her stomach.

"Oh my God," one of the girls said with wild eyes and shaking hands to Myra, clutching at her. "Oh my God!"

The rest of the audience filed in fairly quickly. There were many more girls but a lot of older people too. The stage got busier too, with headphoned technicians walking back and forth. The murmur of the audience was now like the ocean and everyone jumped when a sharp CRACK of a drum behind the curtain went off like a shot. There were nervous scattered titters. Myra wondered if they were already there, behind the curtain, waiting. She wondered if that was Ringo testing his snare drum. It could be. It could be. She was having trouble swallowing now.

Suddenly the room changed. The energy level increased and time and space seemed to shrink. The lights changed, grew brighter and music blared. She could see the titles on the TV monitor right above her and she looked down into her hand and looked at the squished mess of the jelly beans and her Quarter and her multi colored hand.

Suddenly there he was, the man himself, Ed Sullivan standing right in front of her talking about the Beatles. He was wearing a gray suit and was much taller in person. She was telling herself in her mind that hey there was Ed Sullivan right there when suddenly he waved his arm and shouted ".... the Beatles!"

And Myra shrieked.

The keening was a physical thing, a blast as the curtain rose quickly and there they were. The Beatles. Paul, who was already sweating counted fast and began singing "Close your eyes and I'll kiss you/ Tomorrow I'll miss you..."
She was so close that Myra could hear his voice as it went into the microphone. She was so close she could see George's pimples. She was so close that John looked right at her. RIGHT AT HER. He laughed when she screamed. She was so close she could feel the thud of Ringo's drums in her chest, like an extra heart.

Myra was surprised to discover herself screaming, shrieking herself hoarse, tears running down her face, her throat a hard lump. The music came back at them but it was not as powerful. All around her Girls were crying, pleading, reaching without stretched hands. Myra could see Ed Sullivan off to the side, talking out of the corner of his mouth to a woman and smiling a sly snaky smile at the stage.

Myra realized she was being pelted with something; people from the back were throwing things. A yellow jelly bean hit her in the face when she turned to see what it was. It stung and she remembered her own jelly beans and flung them at the stage as hard as she could, her face contorted with such emotion it hardly seemed to be real. All she could see was the Beatles singing their song, her life changing right before her.

She did not know that the cameras had caught her in that moment of throwing her jelly beans and had broadcast her streaked and stricken face into millions of homes, including her own, where her shocked parents watched in amazement at their sweet little daughter's utter and irrevocable transformation. She did not know that the cameras had caught her in that moment of throwing her jelly beans and had recorded for history the greatest moment of her entire life.

Ringo was tapping away at his drums trying to get his mind around the fact that they were in America! And they were just as daft as England when he was volleyed by flying jelly beans. He kept smiling even though he hated the fooking jelly *babies because they fooking hurt you when they hit you in the fooking face.* Something harder than a jellybean hit him the face now and he got mad but he didn't know if he was on camera or not, she he kept smiling. Glancing down he saw the object bouncing on his snare drum. It was an American coin. Ringo saw that it had some old lady engraved on it. He didn't know American money very well yet. Oh well he thought, watching the Quarter dance on his snare drum. At least they're throwing money now.

June 1965
<u>Norsk, INDIANA</u>

It is summer time. Irma is sweeping her porch.

Sweep sweep.

She always sweeps her porch incessantly at this time of day pausing only to stop and rush to her old blond upright piano inside the living room to bang out a few discordant clashes, weep bitterly, then return to the sweeping. In between she fingers and rubs the Quarter inside the pocket of her fading threadbare housedress.

It is her current lucky Quarter. A 1963D. Before there was a 1948S that she mercifully exchanged for an extension cord. The 1948S had been through hell with Irma, who had stroked and fondled it through many life's vicissitudes. Irma's view of luck was mercurial, and she gladly exchanged the 1948S for such a fine black extension cord. Two days later the 1963D was handed to her husband Duke in change for a five-dollar bill when Duke bought his nightly quart of beer.

Irma's criteria for what is to be her lucky Quarter are complicated. It has to do with the weather, the year, the sharpness of the serrated edge, cloud patterns, levels of antioxidants in her bloodstream and a sense of smell that can detect cinnamon from a half mile away. The 1963D was chosen for its shine, high relief and the fact that Irma was sure that George Washington had winked at her when she first examined it.

It is summer time. Irma sweeps her porch.

The heat has not yet risen to full force; there is still a faint crispness and lack of humidity in the air.

Sweep sweep.

She thinks about nothing. And everything. Her mind floats in shards, each reflective and absorbing but unable to fit things together. Like clouds and water or a coin with two sides the same. But different. She rubs the quarter's edge furiously with her calloused finger. Calloused from many years of rubbing the serrated edges of coins.

Rub rub.

Irma hears the souls of the dead crying out and she hears the songs of the birds. It's almost time to play the piano.

Play play.

Almost time to run. Almost time for Duke to come home with his beer, smelling sweet like Roman Catholic incense or a bawdy lady's perfume.

Flash.

Sweep sweep.

Her eccentricities came to Irma in 1951 when she suffered carbon monoxide poisoning. In a freak incident a seat cushion from a TWA airplane was sucked out of a malfunctioning toilet, having been put there by a pre-teen girl and landed right in Irma's chimney, filling her house with noxious fumes. Irma remembered the dreams she had that night, about swimming pools and gray ghosts furiously flying around her, afraid to touch the water. When she was found the next morning by her husband Duke, she was in a coma from which she didn't emerge until three days later. Duke blamed himself because he had been gone all that night. Working he said. Since then, Irma had been scrambled. All the components were there but they were rerouted and their connections sometimes failed to harmonize.

Flash.

She knew it wasn't true, but before she could focus on the thought it melted away and another one replaced it.

Rub rub.

The settlement from TWA was enough for Duke to quit his job as a meat cutter and pursue his dream of being an international spy. At least that's what he said he did. It didn't really matter to Irma. Rub rub.

The serrated edge of the 1963D quarter was slowly being eroded by her friction, sweat and oil. Just like the mountains were eroded by the finger of God. Irma was rigid in her routines, but they consisted of such things as rubbing the quarter, sweeping the porch, pounding tunelessly on the piano, weeping, eating paper, talking to Jesus and avoiding the small baby snakes that emerged from her bath rub faucet every time she turned it on and

Across the street.

Movement.

Irma's heart leapt and her mouth became dry.

Oh no. *Oh no.*

Across the street a squat, scary scruffy man was sitting smoking a cigarette while his two stupid little pug dogs scampered and nuzzled. Of course, Irma did not see stupid little pug dogs but snarling demons, and she kept her head down, heart pounding, sweeping frantically.

Sweep sweep *sweep*.

Rub rub *rub*.

She could hear the pug dogs/demons snuffling and growling and it scared her badly. Orchestras and choirs filled her head; her palms were sweaty in the presence of such danger and evil. She stopped sweeping and with the courage of a lioness she removed the Quarter from her pocket and held it aloft, as if showing the pug dog/demons that she meant business; as if the Quarter was some kind of fearsome magic shield. The sun glinted off of the coin's surface. The pug dogs/demons paid no attention. Nor did their dark master, who sat stroking his beard and smoking cigarettes, the mist and vapors of the Pit surrounding his head like an evil caul.

"Ha! They can't see me! They can't see me now!" Irma was triumphant, her voice carrying across the street. The pug dogs/demons froze and turned their neckless little heads around. Irma thrust the Quarter back into her pocket.

"Ha!" She threw the broom down and stormed into the house, pounding the keyboard of her piano, sounding like a thunderstorm in a wind chime factory.

Play. Play. *Play*.

Feeling better she went back to the front porch to resume the all-important sweeping. She froze at what greeted her. The pug dogs/demons were looking at her now, *looking at her now*! Their lord with his white t-shirt and wing tipped shoes was also looking at her.

They saw her.

Stricken, Irma rubbed the Quarter, took it out of her pocket and kissed it. She solemnly held it out to her audience, as if it could deflect their rays.

Then she popped it into her mouth.

The little pug dogs/demons took off across the street, right toward her house.

Right toward her.

They were coming for her.

Rub rub *RUB*!

She used her tongue.

The man was on his feet, shouting incantations and imprecations.

Irma covered her ears so his words would not invade her soul.

"Goddamn sonofabitch you get your motherfucking asses back here now! Luther! Lucy! Now! Get back here Goddamnit! You stupid worthless little pricks!"

Irma kept her head down, sweeping. It was a busy street, very dangerous for heedless demons and stupid little pug dogs alike. She concentrated on her sweeping.

Sweep sweep.

She heard a car screech, the man howl and then nothing. A second later a car horn. An angry voice.

Sweep sweep *sweep!*

The world was in turmoil and chaos. The end had finally come.

She spat the Quarter out into her hand and replaced it in her pocket. Her saliva was still thick on the surface. The metal tang in her mouth pleased her. Her molecules filled the indentations of the quarter's edge, drying and filling the microscopic pores of its surface, blending in with its composition until they, she and the Quarter, were indistinguishable from one another.

Irma furtively looked up from her sweeping to see the man, who was now revealed to her as Lucifer, slapping and kicking at the badly scared stupid little pug dogs/demons. He picked one up by the collar while the other watched warily. He was yelling and smacking the squirming dog, kicking at the other one to follow him back into his house.

Irma rubbed her lucky Quarter, popped it back into her mouth. She began to weep from the strain and in doing so she hiccupped, swallowing the coin. She choked and gagged but it went all the way down into the soft wet darkness being convulsively moved along like a spaceship in a wormhole to its final destination.

Irma was not unhappy about this turn of events. The Quarter had saved her from Satan and his demons and now would always be with her. Or at least it would be with her for a day or two. The Quarter dreaded the onslaught of stomach acids, but this would not its last time down an alimentary canal. To Irma the universe had been saved by her quick thinking and action. She asked no thanks, just to be allowed in peace to sweep the unbearable beauty that menaced her off of her porch.

Sweep sweep.

August 1966-October 1967

Duke Blime found the Quarter in his wife Irma's bathroom, so he pocketed it and later spent it on a beer at Jug's Tavern.

The Quarter appeared in Decatur Illinois, where it was used in part to purchase the latest 45 rpm record, "Elusive Butterfly" at Main Street records. It was purchased by Susan Oreskevitch along with a small box of Pine scented incense.

The Quarter was given in change to Leonard Pusk, who forgot it in his pants pocket, therefore losing it in the massive clothes dryer at Speedy Laundromat in Wheaton, Illinois.

The Quarter was found in the clothes dryer by Ward Volore an auto mechanic who worked at Sears in Wheaton. It was spent by Volore three days later when he used it in a candy machine to obtain a handful of stale and ancient M&Ms.

The Quarter languished in the candy machine for three months until it was removed and rolled by the owner of the candy machine (and several others in the greater Chicago area) Frankie Esgar. It was then sent to the First National Bank of Chicago where it was redistributed to The First National Bank of Omaha.

The Quarter was dropped on the ground in Mentre, Nebraska by Frank Florax, who did not know he had a hole in his pants pocket. The Quarter lay on the ground until it was found and picked up by Steve Powter, a twelve-year-old boy whose used the Quarter to buy a cigarette off of a teenager named Alex, who had it stolen from him by a boy in school named Craig Curtsy.

October 1967
Pawnee, INDIANA

Impatiently, Craig Curtsy waited for the trick-or-treaters to thin out before he slipped on his mask. It was a plastic face mask, stiff and itchy, that he had bought for three dollars at Duckwalls. It was lashed to his sweaty head by a thin elastic string. The string was held by rapidly tearing holes on the sides of the mask. Inside the mask Craig Curtsy could hear himself breathing.

He had chosen this particular mask at random; it hadn't really mattered for his purposes. It was a Caveman mask, hairy, ridiculous, simian and vaguely threatening. Not that a Caveman was a monster; but the mask turned out to be a stroke of brilliance, with its dull expression; a vaguely disapproving mouth and the white stiffness of the open lifeless eyes. Overall, it projected a whacky, sinister quality that Craig Curtsy had not originally reckoned with.

It was unseasonably warm for Halloween and for that Craig was grateful. He did not want to carry out his mission on a cold night. The idea had struck him like a thunderbolt while watching his favorite show, "Rat Patrol" and he had laughed himself stupid in the Rec room when he imagined its effects. Of course, he told no one. There was no one to tell.

The smells of burning pumpkins and diesel fuel filled Craig Curtsy's head as he set off into the night. The mask shielded him from detection but it also hindered his full range of vision.

Stealthily he crept through blue backyards, jumped over metaphorical fences and cinderblock yard walls, slunk down crunchy alleys, hurried across deserted intersections, all while searching for just the right golden glowing window.

He found it soon enough. It was a brightly lit bay window off an inside dining room facing the back yard of a nicely kept split level home. Craig crept up to the window; whose warm yellow glow made the Caveman mask take on an ominous, grinning beige tone.

The bottom of the window was about level with Craig's shoulders. He peeked around the corner. He could see a family sitting at a dining room table. There was a mother and a father and two small children who were excitedly pouring over their candy haul.

Without thinking, giggling inside the mask, Craig sprung. Using a Quarter, he had stolen from his mom's purse, he tapped loudly at the window and pushed his leering Caveman face up against the glass while moaning as loud as he could. "UNNGGGH! UNGGGHHHAAAHHH!"

In the instant before he bolted, he was treated to their Fear. The father's face was contorted in rage and shock, beet red, a vein throbbing on his forehead, his fists clenched, mouth open bellowing something unintelligible, something harkening back to caveman days, a million years of atavism leapt out of his mouth. The children were screaming, teeth missing in their mouths, their eyes sharp and staring, their hands flailing like flippers. The wife gawked with a non-comprehending stare, her mouth hanging open and her eyes glassy. She was hopping up and down shaking her hands as if they were wet or on fire.

That was all Craig Curtsy had the time to see because he ran as fast as he could, stumbling through the dark choking with laugher and black hearted glee. It was the single greatest moment of his life. It was even better than Craig Curtsy had imagined it would be. When he was safe, he relished the mental picture of their expressions; their hysterical reactions. He laughed again, tears springing into his eyes. He was clutching the Quarter in his hand, conscious not to drop it. Once he caught his breath he searched for a new window.

That night he joyfully reveled the sight of a man throwing his arms up into the air, eyes bulging, false teeth clattering out of his mouth and onto the floor. There was the young couple who he interrupted in the delicate act of lovemaking, both of their faces looking like they just tasted something very sour, the young man's penis popping out of the girl with a jaunty bounce. There was the little boy who shook and wailed, the middle-aged woman who bellowed like a cow and then vomited. There was a party of elderly people who did not react at all, but looked at him with such curiosity that it momentarily confused him. He found a dog to scare. Evidently no one else was at home. He had the dog so worked up it started running desperate circles around the living room, destroying everything in its path.

Craig Curtsy was delirious with happiness and mirth from the scares he was giving his neighbors.

Until he heard the sirens.

He reluctantly threw his disintegrating Caveman mask into some bushes and he ran toward home, careful to use the backyards and carports. The sirens were growing louder as he made his way into the kitchen. He realized he still had the Quarter that was used to tap on their windows in his hand. Hurriedly, he opened the door and threw the Quarter outside. He saw a police car driving slowly down the street sweeping the houses with its spotlight.

Later, Craig Curtsy lay in bed in the room he shared with his brother Scott. Craig was thinking about the faces of the people he had scared. And it made him laugh.

"What's so funny?" Scott demanded.
"Nothing," said Craig Curtsy stowing away those images like shiny silver coins in a treasure chest.

June 1968
Los Angeles, CALIFORNIA

Inez Gallagher was a tiny woman who was being crushed by the crowd. She had begun to regret coming all the way to the to the Ambassador Hotel because she knew someone like her didn't belong there. She just knew she had to be there after what had happened to her at work. She spent her last dollar on bus fare and had only a Quarter left to get herself home.

 But she had to see him.

The chaos of light, the red white and blue of the ballroom was only overpowered by the noisy joy that swept through the hotel after he had been declared the winner. Everything looked different now. Things were going to be righted. Five years ago, a man with a rifle had set the world crooked and now things would go back.

There was a light.

Inez clutched her Quarter, not really knowing why. Her palms were moist and cold, her heart was pounding because she could see that he was coming to address the crowd. Each eye contact was like an unspoken connection, *we are together,* and it was the first time Inez had felt anything like it. She felt her heart unfolding like the opening petals of a flower. People in foam boating hats and red white and blue signs smiled at her and nodded and she smiled too, even though she knew she didn't really belong there.

She was just a motel maid at the Hollywood Inn and was shocked when she went into Suite 2001 and found herself face to face with him. He looked like himself she thought, the mop of unruly hair, the mouth full of expensive Kennedy teeth. His face was heavily lined however. There was none of the television boyishness she had expected. His eyes were like warm coals from a dying fire. He didn't look young up close like this. He looked old and wrinkled. He smiled at her and patted the pockets of his suit coat.

"No, no.." Inez gasped, horrified at the thought of his giving her money.

"Err...uh..." The Senator said and spying a pile of change on the dresser, he bent over, scooping it into his palm and pouring it into her hand. He cupped her hand for her as she gaped and smiling sheepishly, he said in his low famously accented voice, "I don't have any money on me...please take it..."

Again, he smiled a shy, embarrassed smile and she could see now the little boy, the younger brother, and she felt a pull of hope in her chest.

And just as suddenly he was gone. She looked into her palm and saw a bunch of pennies and a Quarter. If it had been anyone else, she would be insulted. But with him, she understood. The room was heavy with his presence. The bed was mussed and the bathroom was still dank and steamy. She collected herself, surprised that a woman her age could be so affected. She had seen movie stars before, but had never felt anything like this. She looked at the coins in her hand again. There was no way she could keep this money.

Now at the podium he was staring into the blazing light, smile dazzling, his thin voice coming from the shrill sound system. There was a hum in the room and the clicking and whirring of cameras was like a Greek Chorus. Inez made her way to the front of the podium just in time to see him give a thumbs up and, as the crowd cheered, he began to walk away from her.

Suddenly, in the swirl of people, he reversed himself and started walking in the opposite direction, right toward her. He edged past well-wishers until he came right upon her, smiling his smile, murmuring *thankyouthankyouverymuch* in his low Boston voice. He grasped her hand but did not squeeze. He looked surprised at the feeling of the Quarter. Inez withdrew her hand and felt something like a current disconnecting.

"Take it...for your campaign. I believe in you." she said loudly into his ear. "It's all I have..." His glowing eyes locked on hers for a split second and he was past her, being rushed into the kitchen area by his people. As they waited for the crowd to clear a path, he had time to glance at the Quarter in his hand, to see that it was a 1963D. That was a tough year, he thought as he walked into the hotel kitchen's teeming crowd and the blinding lights.

August 1969
Bethel, NEW YORK

Jerry Garcia dropped his guitar pick just as the Grateful Dead walked onto the giant plywood stage at Woodstock. The groggy crowd roared its rumbling roar and Jerry was momentarily panicked because he did not have another guitar pick on him.

"Hey man, you got a Quarter?" He asked a hippie standing on the side of the stage, his eyes like prisms. The Hippie blinked and slapped his dirty hands against the dirty white pants he was wearing. Jerry looked out nervously toward the crowd. He was coming down and was ready to play. The August air had a tinge of garbage to it and at times the sound of the cicadas and crickets were like sleigh bells.

The Hippie triumphantly held out a coin for Jerry.

"What year is it?" Jerry demanded. The Hippie blinked and stared at the coin, uncomprehendingly. After a long pause he said, "63. Yeah man. 63."

Jerry nodded and accepted the Quarter. It felt warm and wet from the Hippie's hand. "63 was a passionate year man. The Beatles released their first album the same day Kennedy was shot. Heavy mojo."

The Hippie blinked uncomprehendingly as Jerry smiled and patted him on the shoulder. The crowd suddenly came to life at Chip Monck's introduction, and Jerry moved off toward the sound of an ocean and two very bright white lights.

September 1969
Lake Berryessa, CALIFORNIA

It was dusk on the 27th of September when the Stocky Man finished his work and trudged casually back across the mainly treeless, flat expanse to his car. He could hear the moans and screams but he was unhurried and unconcerned. The Lake was quiet and now, golden hour, it was quite beautiful. There was a breeze picking up the hint of fall and the last of the summer crickets and cicadas ground their legs like jingle bells as the Stocky Man strolled back to where the cars were parked.

The distressed voices had died away in the cool fresh evening but the Stocky Man was sweating beneath his hood and layers of clothes. Taking his time, he removed the hood and threw it in the trunk of his white sedan, which was parked diagonally, Highway Patrol style, behind the cream colored Karmann Ghia.

The Stocky Man listened because he thought he could hear yelling but the breeze kicked up and he heard nothing but the faint, distant *Tatatatatatat* from a woodpecker. He wiped the bloody blade of his bayonet knife on the grass and replaced it in its sheath. He took his pistol and hid it in his trunk. He removed his layers of jackets, used to camouflage his true appearance and pocketed the clip-on sunglasses that he had used on the outside of the hood to obscure his eyes. He could see the hood in his open car trunk, like a lifeless doll, its large square cornered head piece looked like a cloth version of a paper grocery bag with eye holes. The front flap was splayed below the hood and the circle with a cross inside of it he had expertly attached to its center shimmered in the warm glow of the fading sunset.

Closing the trunk, The Stocky Man decided he had had one more chore to perform. He pulled out a magic marker and squatted down next to the boy's Karmann Ghia car. The boy had tried to talk to him during the Event, but he hadn't really listened to him. He was a college boy and talked like a college boy which the Stocky Man despised. It had been a pleasure to stab him. The girl was different, she had squealed which he loved and her desperate fear and animal eyes had excited him past the point of no return.

It had been a good day.

With the magic marker he began writing on the driver's side door of the Karmann Ghia. First, he drew his symbol, the circled cross that looked like a crosshairs in a rifle scope, or a printer's alignment mark or a projectionist's leader symbol. Beneath it he wrote; "Vallejo/12-20-68/7-4-69/Sept 27-69-6:30/by knife."

A sound interrupted him and he stood looking toward the lake. He could see a fishing boat going back and forth near the shore and he thought he heard some shouting

Time to go.

After a leisurely drive of about a half hour toward Napa, The Stocky Man pulled up to a pay phone at the Napa Car Wash. He thought about washing his car after his phone call. He reached into the pocket of his pleated trousers and his fingers felt the change he had taken from the boy when he had told the boy and the girl that he was an escaped convict and needed their money and car keys. It was only about seventy cents, a Quarter and some nickels and pennies. The Quarter had some dried blood on it so the Stocky Man licked it until it was clean then he deposited it into the pay phone.

"Napa Police Department, Officer Slaight."

The Stocky Man at first said nothing.
"Hello?" The Officer sounded annoyed.

"I want to report a murder, no, a double murder. They are two miles north of park headquarters. They were in a white Volkswagen Karman Ghia."

There was a pause while Officer Slaight took this in. "Where are you now?" he asked, his adrenalin rushing.

"I'm the one who did it."

 The Stocky Man almost whispered putting down the phone, careful not to hang it up. He would have liked to have gotten his Quarter back, but sometimes you just had to let that sort of thing go.

July 1970
<u>Houston, TEXAS</u>

Boyd Tang liked to water his lawn. It gave him a sense of accomplishment. The catch was the snakes, who were everywhere in his yard, small black and yellow serpents slithering beneath his feet. It was unnerving.

So, when Boyd Tang watered his lawn he was on alert. His head faced down. When a snake would catch his eye, he would feel his heart jump and the rush of adrenaline. It was an automatic trigger set in place by millions of years of evolution.

It was July and the heat was becoming oppressive. The air outside was heavy and fragrant and in the afternoon crickets and cicadas made their sleigh bell sounds. Bats flapped crazily at dusk, like drunken birds, eating mosquitoes.

As he went outside that day to move his water sprinkler, Boyd tang noticed something other than snakes. He noticed that someone had taken some sort of shovel or tool and had dug an edge around the front part of his lawn. Boyd was not sure if it had been an attempt at vandalism or landscaping. He looked down the street and saw a short, dark man incongruously wearing a jacket and carrying a shovel. He disappeared into the rear of a house a few doors down, back into a converted barn that was now a rental property.

Boyd Tang didn't know how to react. He was outraged that this person had taken it upon himself to alter his lawn at all. But it looked pretty good. Boyd knew that the rental was owned by his landlord, Larry the drill sergeant. Larry was retired from the US

Marines. He liked to tease Boyd about his fear of snakes. One time Boyd had come back from a vacation to find nine headless snakes on his back porch. Compliments of Larry.

Boyd wondered if Larry had perhaps hired this man to do some landscaping at his rental properties. But he quickly dismissed the thought. Boyd reset his sprinkler and returned inside to watch the rest of Lem Rhodesiac's current affairs show. When it was time to move the sprinkler Boyd once again stepped from his air-cooled Frigidaire of a house into the hot cocoon of outdoors.

The man with the shovel looked up from his work and quickly walked away, toward his rental. Boyd, uncertain at first, walked slowly after him. Not wanting the man to feel pursued, Boyd slowly followed his and watched as he returned to his home. Leaving the shovel right outside the door. Boyd examined what the man had been doing. He had edged the entire front of Boyd's yard, making a neat clean line between the grass and the sidewalk. The balance now was more toward outrage rather than admiration for a job well done.

Just then Boyd saw something out of the corner of his eye, move in the grass. His throat tightened and he stepped back in an almost involuntary motion.

It was a snake

 A big one. Black and yellow with a fine head. It stopped and raised that head, looking directly at Boyd, who was frozen on the sidewalk. Regaining his composure, Boyd stamped his foot at the snake, who did not move, but regarded him with what almost seemed like pity. Boyd stamped his foot again, sweat forming on his upper brow. This time the snake did move. It sprang at Boyd, seeming to come off the ground toward him. Charging him.

Boyd jumped back, his mind a universe of fear. The snake came on, slithering onto the hot sidewalk. Boyd ran into the street then around the snake, flanking it until he was behind it. The snake looked around and crawled back into the grass, away from Boyd.

Breathing hard and wet with sweat Boyd Tang felt dizzy. He looked down at the ground and saw a coin; a Quarter, lying just beneath the canopy of grass blades. It was dull and worn but it was still money and Boyd Tang bent to pick it up. As he rose and turned around, he saw the man with the shovel standing on the sidewalk behind him.

The man was dapper and balding. He was dressed in many layers of clothes which struck Boyd as odd on such a hot day. The man regarded Boyd with what almost seemed like pity. Boyd was ashamed and looked into his hand. He was turning the quarter around and around. On an impulse he held it out for the man. The man took it and began edging the sides. Boyd decided to go back into his air-conditioned house to look for something cold to drink.

(Withheld) 1971
The Moon

The hatch of the lunar module hissed as it opened, a few puffs of leftover water vapor escaped toward them in a sparkling white cloud that rapidly dissolved like tiny fireworks in the vacuum of space. Astronaut (*Withheld*) was very tired. They had been on the moon for over two hours and it had been a surreal dream like experience.

Astronaut (*Withheld*) wondered if there even was such a thing as reality anymore.

Astronaut (*Withheld*) had performed all of his mission tasks, working efficiently. He saw to some photographs, the core samples, rock collecting and setting up the seismometer, the ultra violet ray collector, the flag, among many other tasks. The Astronauts had to work briskly. This was the money time and they needed to go home with something to show for it. He was aware of what was happening and where he was, but it didn't really feel real to him.

Astronaut (*Withheld*) wondered if there even was such a thing as reality anymore.

 He could look up into the black velvet sky, a sky so back that he didn't understand the meaning of the word black until now. He would stare at the Earth, which looked like a drop of water suspended in the night, lit from within like a charming Christmas ornament. He tried to wrap his mind around the fact that he was outside of his planet. To him, it was all just what it was. He didn't try to understand it too much. When he went there, he felt his mind and soul suddenly on the verge of something very large and very scary, just beyond the point of what he was able to understand about anything.

Astronaut (*Withheld*) wondered if there even was such a thing as reality anymore.

He was concentrating on these final few moments on the moon, knowing that nothing like this would ever happen to him again in his life. He wanted to remember. He wanted to imprint everything he saw and felt in his mind so he could recall it perfectly when he got back. He didn't know then that it would be like trying to recreate the intensity of a dream.

He stared intently at his footprints in the ashy powder of the lunar soil. As his partner struggled up the LEM's ladder into the open hatch, Astronaut (*Withheld),* reached into his rock bag and withdrew his own personal treasure that he had smuggled all the way from Houston. It was a roll of Quarters, not shiny new ones, but old ones from all over. Astronaut (*Withheld*) did not like shiny new coins. He liked to think about the journeys that these Quarters had made and how he had extended their journeys far beyond that of other, unluckier coins.

Because it was impossible to bend over in his pressure suit, Astronaut (*Withheld*) knelt and carefully opened the top of the plastic tube that contained the Quarters. He carefully scooped some lunar soil into the tube, coating the coins within in a thin layer of gray gunpowder smelling dust.

Astronaut (*Withheld*) wondered if there even was such a thing as reality anymore.

His partner was almost through the hatch now and soon it would be his turn. Astronaut (*Withheld*) replaced the dusty tube of Quarters in his rock bag. He could sell them for a thousand dollars each when he got back to Texas. Maybe even pay off his house and buy a new set of decent golf clubs. The gray dusty ash-like dirt was all over everything. Looking up he again saw the Earth, in crescent, and his heart pounded as if he had just seen his lover.

Astronaut (*Withheld*) wondered if there even was such a thing as reality anymore.

November 1970-April 1971

The Quarter was returned to Earth and was given to a cocktail waitress named Lena Todd Thomas who worked at Whisky Dick's, a bar in southern Cocoa Beach, Florida. Lena Todd Thomas, who was told that this very Quarter had been to the moon, didn't believe the man who gave it to her, or that he even was a real Astronaut, so she spent the Quarter in a candy machine a week later. Lots of guys said they were astronauts where she worked.

The Quarter reentered circulation from a Savannah Georgia bank, where it was distributed to a Piggly Wiggly store in Brungberg, Georgia. It was given in change to Kilde Hocking who kept it in a plate on his dresser until he needed it to buy cigarettes.

The Quarter next appeared in Rile, Texas, where it was used by Randy Swerdfenger to buy stamps from a post office machine to mail in some song lyrics, he had written to a company who would put his lyrics to music. The name of his song was "Fat Dog in America."

The Quarter was given in change at the Post Office to Martin Musto, who was driving home from his father's funeral in Austin.

April 1971
Pueblita, ARIZONA

Eleven-year-old Frankie Musto waited impatiently in the examining room while the technicians developed his X-rays. His eyes covered everything, imprinting it all on his mind. He sought out the corners and the edges, the tiny spider webs in the windows, the beckoning drawers and thick white expensive looking machines. He had broken his wrist two weeks earlier by jumping up to grab a tree branch. He swung his body out and lost his grip, falling with his left arm flush against his chest.

Crack!

Frankie's mother was so pissed that she snarled at him in the car, "If that goddamn arm isn't broken, I'm going to break it myself!" Fortunately for Frankie it was indeed a compound fracture. Now he didn't have to do dishes for eight weeks! "You're pretty goddamned happy for someone with a broken arm," his mother said.

Indeed, Frankie happily adjusted to life in an arm cast. It suddenly made him a celebrity at school. All the kids wanted to write something on it. People who had never given him another glance now smiled at him. Girls ran their sleek young hands along its hard surface, blushing and giggling. It soon became a multicolored fingerprint smudged canvas of peace signs, imprecation, witticisms, caricatures and signatures. It went from brilliant white to a dirty yellow bone color. It began to smell like an unfortunate combination of sweaty feet and onions. It was time for a new one.

A nurse entered the room followed by a doctor. The nurse was young with frizzy hair. She was skinny and sun tanned. Her eyes were full of alarm. She was carrying a heavy lead apron. The doctor was an older man with a bald head. He looked angry in his eyes which bored into Frankie as if he would read his mind about rifling the drawers a second ago. Their faces were pinched.

"Did you lodge something in that cast? Like a coin? Say a nickel or a Quarter?" The doctor threw the accusation out like a fastball. Both he and the nurse stood back to see its effect. Frankie's mom, standing in the doorway behind them said, "Goddamnit Frankie..."

"It's really quite dangerous and this Quarter for whatever reason blew out the tube in the x-ray machine. It's as if this Quarter was exposed to quite a bit of radiation prior to the x-ray..."

Frankie blinked. What did they mean? He opened his mouth. As he did the doctor whipped out the x-ray and held it up to the light.

"I... I..."

There was Frankie's broken wrist in all its cracked glory. The cast looked like a faint shroud enveloping it. Right over the cracked bone was the shock of an opaque disk.

"You should have told us before we x-rayed it," the Nurse blurted, her voice full of fear.

"Goddamnit Frankie..." His mother said.

"Looks like a nickel. Might be a Quarter." The doctor said disapprovingly, revving up the saw.

August 1971
<u>Menke, OHIO</u>

Ben Prittenger was eager to walk to Duckwalls Dime Store to spend his allowance. Each week he got two dollars, which his father handed to him in change from the jar on his dresser. Ben often raided the jar when his father was not around, but at this juncture, his father didn't know it.

For now, though, it was summer, delicious summer in Menke, the smell of brackish water in the baking cement gutter, hot asphalt and wet dirt and the green of a million living plants and trees blended together to make Ohio in the summer. Ben had a Quarter, four dimes and six nickels, left from his weekly two dollars and this being Sunday, he decided to treat himself to a quart of strawberry Shasta and the new MAD magazine.

Duckwalls was about a half mile away, straight down Bay State Road. Like Ben, all the other neighborhood kids threw their candy/record/magazine business their way. Menke didn't have too many places for kids to spend their allowances since the mica mines closed. Ben was old enough now, at the age of eleven, to begin to understand the social and economic strata he occupied. As he made the walk, Ben noticed that each block he passed got a little seedier. The houses seemed to sag and sigh more, some leaning oddly to one side or the other. The yards went from well-groomed green lushness to dusty and brown, with engines and anvils on the porches and dogs tied up, lying on their sides in the shade.

Ben was walking fast down the street, there was no sidewalk, and rather than paying attention, (Bay State was a busy road,) he was performing a concert in his head. Today he was Elton John, singing "Take Me to The Pilot" half out loud and thanking the imaginary audience for their fervor with his odd Ohio approximation of a British accent.

He passed a sprawling tract house with a big chain link fence, gated at the driveway. The fence was six feet tall and the gates were slightly ajar. On the other side of the fence a large black German Shepard suddenly went berserk, barking furiously and hurling itself at the fence. Ben remembered this dog and was grateful for the fence because it seemed like it had definite personality issues. This time, however, when the snarling snapping dog threw itself against the gate, the gate swung open.

Ben saw the gate open and the black blur rocket toward him, the barking increasing in tempo and pitch. Ben ran, he ran as he had never run before, easily out running the dog. He didn't know where he was going to go, but he was running. He briefly thought he could make it home, but he realized that he couldn't maintain this level of speed indefinitely. He could hear the dog behind him in furious pursuit, barking and growling, and his heart pounded with panic and fear.

Suddenly the dog was gone and the echoes of a whistle lingered in the air. Ben eased up and looked back to see a man in an army fatigue jacket calling the dog back. He slammed the gate and started running toward Ben, who had stopped in the middle of Bay State road and as panting with shock and fear.

The man in the green fatigue jacket was suddenly upon him. He seized Ben by the arm and jerked him toward the gates. The dog was pacing back and forth barking and whining and chewing on the steel mesh of the chain link fence. Ben's fear spiked as he looked into the man's eyes. They blazed with anger, but were glassy and watery as well. He was shaggy and unshaven but his posture was ramrod straight. His fatigue jacket told Ben he had just come back from Vietnam but Ben didn't know if that was really true. Suddenly the man slapped Ben across the face and shook him by the shoulders and hissed in his face with breath that smelled like beer and cigarettes.

"You little prick! You let my dog out on purpose! That dog would have killed you!" He slapped Ben again. Hard. Ben was shocked, not least of all because it was not the truth.

"I didn't! I swear! He jumped at the gate and it came open!" Ben started crying.

"You fucking little liar." The Man slapped Ben again. It stung, but his face was already turning numb. "I fuckin' saw you do it!"

Ben didn't know what to say to this. He knew any further denials would likely be met with another blow. But he couldn't help himself.

"I didn't! I swear!"

The Man did not slap him this time but seized him by the front of his shirt, like they do in movies, and picked him up so their faces were almost touching.

"You slimly little fuck. If that dog had caught you, you'd be dead by now. One word from me and he'll tear you to pieces..."

"Pleeaase..." Ben sobbed now, waiting for it to be over.

"You got any money?" The Man demanded suddenly, disturbingly calm. "You put my purebred dog in danger. That entitles me to compensation. If you don't have any money then I have to take my compensation in some other way."

"All I have is this Quarter," Ben whimpered, offering it to the Man who was chewing on the inside of his mouth and speaking through clenched teeth. He took the Quarter and put it in the front pocket of his fatigue jacket. The name on the patch above the left breast said "Asgar."

"It's not the amount but the gesture." The Man said. When Ben didn't answer, the Man seemed to grow angry again.

"I know you," the Man went on, spitting in Ben's face. Their eyes were locked together and all other sound and life ceased around them. "I know where you live. I know where you sleep. If I ever see you walk by here again, I'll come see you real late some night and maybe cut your fucking throat."

The Man released Ben, shoving him backwards so that he staggered and fell onto the ground. The Man grinned an unsettling, dangerous grin and spun around, calling his dog. He looked at Ben again and threw the Quarter down into the street, then pointed to it. Ben leaned over and picked it up, confused. The man grinned again, this time to himself, without looking at Ben, like they shared a secret now, and then he walked back into the house without once looking back at Ben.

After composing himself, Ben decided to go home. He didn't feel like MAD magazine or strawberry Shasta anymore. Even if he did still have his Quarter. He was careful to take the long way back so as to bypass the entire block. He walked in shock. The trees buzzed with June bugs and birds and the traffic was extra loud and aggressive sounding. Every step he took he looked back to see if he had been followed. On the way back he didn't sing even a single song.

January 1972
<u>Springsteen, West Virginia</u>

The leafless trees swayed with the cold winds, their knobby branches like spindly arms in a school play. The sky was January white and heavy yet it really wasn't that cold outside. But it was cold enough. It was one of those nights that was just like in the movies, forbidding and ominous and smelling like old dry onions.

Especially in a cemetery, which neighbored vast stubbled onion fields.

And here was Martin Morrison and Gary Jubal, two teenage boys carrying crowbars, their trendy oversized Vibram-soled hiking boots leaving strong identifiable imprints in the grassless dirt of the unsodded fresher graves. Martin and Gary looked like puffballs in their fashionable goose down coats, but no one was there to see them so they didn't care. Martin had already torn his coat and little white feather leaked from it as they made their way through the rows of headstones toward mausoleum row. The goose down coats had been Christmas presents, as had been the suede hiking boots that everyone at County High had to have that holiday season.

They had jumped the iron fence at Sacred Martyrs Catholic Cemetery just outside of town. They were not there to randomly vandalize or dig up any old grave. They knew exactly where they were going. The wind was blowing a storm in, and maybe it would even snow, but it felt too warm to really snow. The sky was so white it felt like a circus tent with a bright light shining above it through the canvas.

"This way." Gary said into the wind, careful not to turn on his flashlight lest someone spot them from the road.

"Gary maybe we..."

"Go home then pussy!" Gary wheeled on Martin. His eyes were blazing.

Martin hung his head in shame.

Two days before Gary had read in the paper about a girl their age who was killed in a car crash. They had published her picture in the paper and Gary had been struck and then mesmerized with her. Right away he knew that this was not just some stupid infatuation with some girl whose picture he saw somewhere. This was a deep and abiding love that was whole and pure and had sprung on Gary unbidden, unwanted and unattainable. Her face was all he could think of night and day. It haunted him, burned itself into his mind. When he shut his eyes, it became animates, mouthing his name, smiling at him, the eyes blinking.

The fact that the girl, whose name was Felicity Gomez, was dead, did not phase Gary who immediately called his best friend Martin to tell him about her. Martin, not realizing at first Gary was talking about a dead girl, asked Gary when he could meet her. And maybe did she have a friend for him.

"I'm working on it." Gary had said.

The next thing Martin knew they were at a funeral at Holy Family church and Gary was wearing a brick red leisure suit his mom had gotten him at Sears. Martin went along because he had never seen a dead body before, but much to their consternation the casket was closed for the funeral. The service was brief, with Father Chan droning on about lost opportunities and God's everlasting disapproval.

Later, at the reception in the basement of Holy Family, Gary introduced himself and Martin to Felicity's stunned and benumbed parents a friend of hers, even being so bold as to insinuate that they had been more than friends. Trying to appear knowing with a mouthful of cake wasn't working too well for Gary and Martin was getting nervous.

There was increasing whispers and dirty looks from the other teenagers there, most of whom went to Central High with Felicity instead of County High where Martin and Gary went.

"We should go," Martin whispered to his friend as a tall boy in a letter jacket shot them a hard look and began to make his way toward them from across the basement hall.

"Screw them, I have just as much right to be here as they do. She was my girlfriend." Gary was defiant. Martin wondered of his friend had gone crazy.

"I'm tired of it Martin. I'm tired of not having a girlfriend. Of not ever having kissed a girl or touched a girl or having been touched by a girl. I'm finished. This is my way out."

Outside at twilight the grayness of January had never been more evident or oppressive. Even a sunset couldn't add any color. The gray just sucked it all in and thinned it out until it only made the gray a little brighter, a little heavier.

Gary and Martin stood hunched on a doorway of Holy Family sharing a lemon scented cigarette Gary had stolen from his mother's purse.

"Man, what are we doing here?" Martin was shivering in his thin jean jacket.

"I gotta have her," Gary said, his eyes glittering. "She's all mine now."

"What do you mean? What are you going to do Gary? You want to dig her up and keep her in your room?" Martin laughed derisively but Gary remained unsmiling.

"Among other things." He said quietly.

Martin thought a minute. Gary knew he was thinking because he was biting his lower lip.

"I don't know man," Martin tried, testing Gary's resolve. Gary struck back viciously.

"Screw you then faggot! I don't need your help. I thought you would be the one who would understand but screw you! "

Martin hung his head in shame. Gary threw the wet lemon cigarette out into the parking lot of Holy Family church. The wind was picking up and it was getting dark. They watched as the fleet of black Cadillacs slowly drove out of the lot and onto the street. They watched the red taillights, all lined up, all the way down the street.

So now five hours later they were in the cemetery, two crowbars, the wind and dead trees. A perfect setting. Gary didn't even recognize it.

"I just gotta have her," he kept saying. "She's all mine now."

"How are you going to keep her in your room? I mean how are you going to keep your mom from finding her?

"I don't know," Gary said. "All I know is that she is going to belong to me."

"That's kind of sick Gary."

"No, what's sick is the game girls play, the way they taunt you and the way they look you over to pick the best one, the best boy they can find. I mean what's so wrong with me? I'm normal. I like stuff. Why do they just look at me and then look somewhere else? Felicity won't look away from me Martin. She can't."

"It's just not right."

"I don't care. Go home pussy. faggot. We don't need you."

Martin hung his head in shame.

Luckily for them, they had not buried Felicity Gomez in the cold cold ground, but had interred her in a family crypt, above ground like many of the more recent graves in this cemetery. Due to the coal seams and hollows underground, burial was not entirely advisable in these parts.

This was a lucky break for Gary and Martin who never could have gotten six feet under the ground and then dealt with a concrete vault. As it was, they had a hard enough time breaking into the vault, which was basically a cement cube with decorative columns. It was surrounded by fresh flowers staked to the surrounding ground and fluttering in the wind. They added a discordant note of sweetness to the gray January night with its wind and its heavy white sky.

Using the crowbars, they went to work on the freshly sealed door. Since the mortar had not had time to properly set it was relatively easy for even these two to work the slab aside and gain entry into the tomb.

Inside they used flashlights to see a stark bare space with three coffins. There were dead flowers and old wreaths on the floor along with the fresh ones left earlier that day. Two of the coffins were huge and metal looking, they were covered by a fine layer of dust which the wind blew in little particles to dance in their flashlight beams.

The coffin they were looking for was almost blonde in color, and smaller than they had expected. It was new and shiny and Martin noticed that Gary's hands trembled as he pulled off the carpet of flowers and rubbed his hand over the polished smooth curved cover.

Martin was getting scared now, the sight of the coffins had done it.

"Let's go!" He hissed but Gary just waved him off. Martin started backing out of the little room and Gary wheeled, shining the beam of his flashlight right into Martin's face. Gary said nothing. Martin hung his head in shame. Gary turned back to the coffin. She was in there; he could feel it. He frantically searched for a way to open the coffin lid. Martin watched him, wondering if he ever really knew his friend at all. He did not really recognize this person. He was thrilled and repulsed, kind of like when he heard his parents having sex.

"It's gotta be here somewhere." Gary said and he turned to look at Martin with such a look of desperation that Martin came forward to help his friend. He felt around the lower edge of the lid and found what felt like a latch. He pulled at it and something sprung hard. The sound reverberated throughout the room.

Now they both were shaking as they tried to play the beam of their lights into the coffin. Gary raised the lid, which did not creak like they do in movies, but hissed, like something hydraulic. It was heavy and lined with white, like the sky outside.

Inside the coffin was Felicity Gomez, dressed in her pink tufted satin prom dress, her hands holding a rosary. Her perfect fingernails were painted white. Little mementoes filled the sides of the coffin, little stuffed animals, some friendship bracelets, beaded necklaces, some coins, some notes, some pictures.
What finally made Gary step back in horror was her head, which was wrapped in a white sheet covered by heavy clear plastic. Her head looked like a giant soap bubble.

Martin reached into the coffin and grabbed a handful of the change. Some pennies and a Quarter. He was just turned around when the little room was suddenly filled with a very bright light and the very loud indignant sounds of unforgiving retribution.

September 1973
Laurel, Maryland

"Oh, I have an eye appointment Friday. Help me remember."

"Okay. (Pause) You know, you have an eye appointment on Friday. Don't forget to remember."

"Goofball! Remind me on Thursday!"

"Okay remind me to remind you on Thursday."

"I'll just call the house and leave a message on the answering machine."

"It's about time we got our money's worth out of that thing."

"Can you give me a dime so I can call from that pay phone?"

"All I have is a Quarter."

"Well remind me to pay you back when we get home."

"Okay. (Pause) Hey don't forget to give me my Quarter back when we get home. I was going to buy some shoelaces with it."

"That is what the problem is! I cannot remember to remind you!"

"Remind me about what?"

October 1973-February 1974

The Quarter was used in various vending machines, slowly working its way north. It was used to buy cigarettes in Pennsylvania, a pack of gum in New York, a condom in Michigan. A succession of coin boxes.

The Quarter was given as the only Christmas present to Bennie Evans age eleven. Bennie lived in the worst slum of Detroit, and this was the first Christmas present he had ever gotten. It seemed like so much money to him that he couldn't decide how to spend it. He hid it beneath the wallpaper by his bed while he thought about what to do with it. Because of this indecision, his brother Chico stepped in and stole the Quarter from the wallpaper while Bennie slept and lost it in a craps game the next day.

The Quarter was used in a juke box by Chico Evans at Randy's Roadhouse Bar and Grill at 1066 East Addison in Milwaukee Wisconsin. The selection was a song called "Jug Pumpin'" by the Neotastics. This particular song was chosen to impress a woman named Iona Benavidez. It did not succeed.

The Quarter reentered circulation and was part of a weekly pay packet for Guy Farwl, who added it to the Hansen's Peanut butter stash jar he kept hidden in his bedroom closet. He was hoping to save up enough change to buy some golf shoes.

February 1974
Spang, WISCONSIN

Cri de Coeur.

That maddening phrase ran through Andrew's head like a mantra as he awoke. He had read it in a book of his mom's; a witchcraft book, as that was her latest fad. He was reading about the desperate howl of werewolves.

Cri de Coeur.

It meant "cry from the heart."

Emerging from sleep Andrew could hear voices. In the other room. Everyone else was up. He had slept late. Very late and no one had awakened him for school. A heaviness hit him and his stomach knotted with shame and fear.

"Did your mother tell you about Andrew?" He heard his father say. He didn't hear his sister's reply. Only the subdued and frightened tone of her voice. In that moment it all came crashing back down upon him.

Cri de Coeur.

It was that awful moment of realization after a life changing previous day. The weight of it all suddenly pressed down on Andrew like a million stones. Like being pressed to death by Puritans. He wanted to stay in bed forever. he just wanted to sleep.

Andrew was only fourteen and already his crimes had made him a hopeless case; someone who knew that his entire life had been ruined by one wrong decision. His heart pounded and his stomach clenched at the thought of having to face everyone after what had happened yesterday. He heard the shrill voice of his brother and the rustle of the paper his father was reading. He could smell the coffee and the cigarette smoke, smells of morning that now made him sick with regret and apprehension.

Yesterday was like every other day. Andrew had come home from school and parked himself in front of the TV for the Gilligan's Island/Leave it to Beaver hour. His father had come home from his job as a butcher at Safeway, blood spattered and angry, and went in to take his shower, just like he always did. When he was finished with his shower he went into his bedroom and closed the door. After just a few minutes in his bedroom, he called out.

"Andrew!" His voice was sharp, but it cracked. It cracked in a way that gave Andrew a very bad feeling. He went to his father's bedroom. He passed the bathroom still billowing soapy shower steam, Old Spice and shit. When he reached the bedroom, he saw his dad standing almost comically, with a towel wrapped around his belly. His white hair was disarranged. His eyes were red and unblinking. On the bed was the jar.

It was a Hansen's peanut butter jar, economy size that was full of change and the odd dollar bill or two. It was his father's stash jar. Andrew 's heart pounded harder. His father pointed at the jar like a man pointing to a snake.

"Have you been taking my money? Have you been stealing my money?" His father asked him in a barely-under-control tone that Andrew had only heard a few times before. Andrew 's mind raced. He automatically went to deny it but his father shifted his head, silently daring him to deny what he already knew to be the truth.

Andrew closed his mouth, looked at the jar and nodded. He looked at all the silver change he had left in the jar. He had always been careful to take just a little so it wouldn't be noticed. But like any addiction just a little was never enough. He had been dipping into it pretty liberally as of late. It all started when he saw a bin of cut out 45s at Tempo. He found several rare David Bowie records as well as some early T-Rex. He had treated himself to burgers and generally used it as walking around money. Things had been going great. Records were his life; they were the only thing that meant anything to him. To find such a stash and not have any money to buy it was torture. Right or wrong never entered into it.

"I've been counting it," his father said, pinning Andrew with his unblinking, bloodshot eyes. "I know every cent you took from there. You took over thirty dollars. That was my money. Money I was saving..."

At this his father flew into action, seizing Andrew by the arm and shaking him violently. He humiliatingly spanked Andrew as if he was a small boy, but the blows didn't register, only the red-faced rage in his father's face and the laser like heat from his eyes made an impression on Andrew. His father hit him again and again, his voice coming loud through tightly clenched teeth.

".... saving for GOLF SHOES! I can abide anything but a thief!
And that's all you are is a thief!"

He stopped hitting Andrew and pushed him away in disgust.
Andrew could see his father was barely in control. Tears ran down
his face. Andrew was crying too as was his little brother who had
toddled in and witnessed the scene. His father grabbed him again
and Andrew thought he was going to hit him but instead his father
made a hideous sound from the back of his throat. A sound that
immediately made a phrase pop into Andrew 's head and lodge
itself there.

Cri de Coeur.

A cry from the heart.

"Why didn't you just ask me?" His father asked him brokenly.
"Why did you have to steal?"

"I'm sorry..."

His father's anger flashed. "You're just sorry you got caught." His
father was right. Andrew felt nothing for stealing the change. He
had needed that money and whenever he did work up the nerve to
ask his father, the answer was always no. Those records had meant
everything to him. He had memorized the labels, examined the run
off grooves, he would watch them as they went round and round
on the turntables. How could his father understand that?

"Go and bring me every single thing you bought with that money
because it's mine." His father said breathing heavily, lighting a
cigarette.

Andrew walked past his snuffling brother into his room. In shock
he opened his top drawer and began pulling out random things, A
kazoo. A pocket knife. A yoyo. A set of wacky clackers. He kept

this up until he had what he thought was thirty dollars' worth of stuff. It never occurred to him to actually give back the records he bought with the stolen money. He would never give up those records.

"Where's the rest of it?" His father demanded, looking at the pitiful accumulation of loot. "I... I bought some burgers..." Andrew said but a look from his father silenced him. Sighing, blowing out smoke he looked at Andrew again. Andrew could see all the disappointment, all the fury, all the betrayal in his father's eyes. *Cri de Coeur.*

"Not much here. Just a bunch of shit. You sold my trust and respect for you pretty cheap." His father threw the cigarette down and without another word walked back into the bathroom and slammed the door. Andrew heard his hot comb going as he lay down on his bed, fear soaked and ashamed, and fell deeply and instantly asleep.

"Andrew!" His mother's voice made him sit up in bed. "You're going to be late for school!" Andrew got up and got dressed as slowly as possible. He did not want to go into the kitchen. He did not want to face anyone. But he did. His brother and sister had been laughing and fighting but when he walked into the room, they fell silent. His father continued reading the paper, ignoring him.

Andrew walked through the kitchen to get ready for school. His sister did likewise. She glanced at him quickly as if to gauge the depth of his pain and shame and taking the tiniest of sips, she seemed satisfied.

"Oh Daddy! It's ice cream sandwich day! Can I have a quarter to take to school?" His sister ran over to him. He fished in his pocket and withdrew some change. He handed her a quarter, then he held one out for Andrew to take. Andrew shook his head.

"Take it." His father said, looking Andrew in the eyes. Andrew walked over and took the Quarter. He let his hand touch the fingers of his father. They were rough and cold. The Quarter passed between them and things would never be the same. Andrew vowed to himself that he would never spend that Quarter. He would save it and someday he would give it to his son; just give it to him for no reason.

July 1974
Berne, IOWA

Nancy Drew took a lot of shit about her name. It wasn't even her real name, she was adopted. She didn't know what her real name was, but Nancy Drew just never felt right to her. She felt more like a Carla or a Valerie than a Nancy. But what could you do?

Nancy Drew could not see in color. Dr Pierce, the highest paid optic surgeon in Cedar Rapids said there was no good reason why she couldn't see in color. She just couldn't. She once asked her father to describe the color blue to her and after a long moment he said, "cold." Try it. It isn't so easy.

Nancy was driving on Rural Road 2717 just outside of Berne, on her way home from the Fourth of July with her mother. She knew she would be coming to a junction soon where there was a toll road so she started rummaging through her purse looking for a couple of Quarters.

Just outside of Herb Kramer's hog field, Nancy's attention was snagged by a large, circling bird. Then another one. There was a spot-on Nancy's windshield as she drove and she couldn't help but force herself to focus on it. The spot seemed to pulsate and branch out, like the history of rivers and Nancy was mesmerized by it. One part of her mind was sharp; pay attention to the road, but she felt frozen within; suddenly in a place so beautiful she never wanted to leave.

Nancy glanced at the road and noticed she was weaving. The Quarters felt hot and wet in her hand. There was a groaning sound and Nancy was suddenly weightless, one of the Quarters flying into her face and chipping her tooth. Everything was flying upside down. Nancy was calm as she realized the car was going end over end. Hmm. She thought. So, this is what it's like to be in a car wreck. She was oddly serene and slightly bemused that nothing seemed to be touching her. Nothing was hurting her. It was almost like an amusement park ride.

The car settled several hundred feet away from the road, right side up in a drainage ditch. Nancy was outside the car somehow and she guessed she was in shock. She had no memory of climbing out of the car or of being thrown clear, but here she was, standing by the side of her wrecked car, unhurt and unscathed.

Her car was another matter. It was a ball of twisted metal and chrome, smoking and chugging, the engine still idling in a clanky, broken way. She kept testing herself over and over again. Making sure she wasn't hurt anywhere. Despite some stiffness however, she was fine. Almost euphoric. She was dreamy and elated that she had survived. Things seemed so much more vivid and alive. The evening stars were ten times brighter, the sounds were suddenly shards of sensation in her ears that made her back tingle and her throat hurt. She could smell the earth; she could smell it all, an unimaginable cornucopia of deliciousness.

She knelt in the ditch and touched the muddy bank to make sure she wasn't a ghost. The dirt moved at her touch and she was reassured. Relieved. It was fine and cool and she knew that it was everything that had ever lived before.

Then she realized.

Color.

Technicolor.

Vista Vision.
Vista-Vision.

She hadn't processed it before this but all of a sudden, she could see in color. She was flash flooded with emotion but it burned off quickly, leaving her feeling strangely nonchalant, distant from her own feeling, as if something inside was receding.

She tried dancing around halfheartedly in celebration, as she had seen people on TV do. She supposed that this was the proper way to react to something like this, but she didn't really feel like it though.

She stopped dancing when she saw the tree that had stopped her car from going further into Herb Kramer's hog field. She had never before seen anything so beautiful. It was a universe; and it was wounded and dying. Her car had opened a gash in the tree that would ultimately prove fatal.

Filled with remorse, Nancy Drew caressed the tree and felt its life ebb away and she cried and watching the brilliant night endlessly unfold treasure at her shoeless feet. Nancy drew in a breath and the cold air filled her head and made it swim. She let the other Quarter fall from her hand onto the ground, she didn't need it anymore. So, this was the world. Her car hissed and smoked and she threw it a sorrowful glance when she thought she saw something trying to move inside.

January 1975
Lansing, MICHIGAN

Ripper the dog died after eating a Quarter which had lodged in her throat choking her to death. Steve Latino buried her in the backyard the next morning. He felt nothing for Ripper, or any dog for that matter, but especially Ripper. Steve Latino was not aware that in Ripper's coma, her life replayed itself like a grand dog opera. Ten years is a long time for a dog, and her story was almost biblically epic and it unwound for any interested enough to bother to tune it in.

Ripper was born in 1965 and as a puppy came into the possession of Steve Latino's sister Tammy. Ripper was a rambunctious puppy who liked to tear things with her teeth; but this wasn't why Tammy named her Ripper. Tammy named her Ripper because of a certain gastrointestinal problem that the German Shepard mix was subjected to throughout her life. This enraged Steve Latino's father, Arthur, who hated Ripper, but still liked the dog more than the fucking cats.

This little puppy chewed and farted on everything in sight, especially Arthur's golf shoes. But before Arthur Latino could make good on his grim promise to shoot Ripper in the head, he dropped dead of a heart attack on the second tee, just after hitting a two iron onto the green.

Ripper's life was spared then and from that point the dog seemed to lead a charmed existence. As she grew, Steve too, came to hate her. Not because of any personal animosity, for Ripper was always the friendliest of dogs, but because Ripper had chosen the basement Rec room for her favorite toilet, a Rec room that Steve Latino had to cross daily like a stinking minefield, to get to his room. Every morning he would open his door and the stench of stale dog shit would hit him with full force. It was the first inclination in his life that he might one day want to kill another living being.

His mother and his sister had long ago abandoned the basement to Ripper and Steve until it got so bad Steve decided to move out and join the army. This was to escape the dog shit more than anything else and he hoped he'd never have to see Ripper again.

Tammy Latino moved out of her mother's house shortly thereafter, when their mother went crazy and began spending all her time in Gay bars trying to save people's souls for Christ. Tammy took Ripper with her to Lansing, where Tammy hoped to get her degree in the funeral arts.

It was in Lansing, that Ripper had the first of her adventures. When Ripper was three, Tammy's friend Cindy Shune was babysitting Ripper while Tammy was at a post mortem extreme reconstruction seminar in Eau Claire. Cindy Shune was not known for her intelligence; the pentagram tattooed to her forehead was evidence of that.

So, while she had the use of Tammy's house for a week, she decided to use it to her advantage to make a few extra bucks. Since Ripper always barked at strange men, Cindy locked the dog in the bathroom while she took care of business. Also, in the bathroom, in the tub, was a cardboard box full of mewling kittens Cindy had found outside Swanks.

When the men had left for that night, Cindy opened the bathroom to let Ripper out and was greeted by the bloody mess of tangled dead kittens and a friendly looking Ripper, tail wagging, gore and fur all over her muzzle.

Tammy was urged by all who knew her to have Ripper put down, but she resisted because she knew Ripper was not responsible for the deaths of the kittens, but she never again allowed Ripper to "kiss" her; the notion of kitten blood and guts on Ripper's jaws was just too much for her to take.

Things went on for the next couple of years, with Ripper having her first litter of puppies and Tammy settling down to a job specializing in embalming babies and children at Addams Mortuary in Lansing. It was during this time that Tammy met her husband, Roy, and when they got married, they did the smart thing, leaving Ripper in a kennel instead of with Cindy Shune when they went on their honeymoon cruise up the Detroit River.

This was the Dark Time in Ripper's life. The prison was cold and she was in a cramped cage all day, covered in her own shit, unable even to stand, barking herself hoarse. She broke two teeth on the wire cage, but her practiced jaws told her that with a little work, the impossible could be possible.

After four days of incarceration, Ripper managed to escape from the kennel on the very day Tammy and Roy were due back from their cruise. It was not from chewing through the cage though, that Ripper made her escape. She simply charged the dumb girl who took her out once a day to hose out the cage and give her some food and water. Ripper could see that the back door was open. She could see a clear path to daylight and the only thing in her way was a girl who was afraid of her.

Ripper had never run so fast. As the cinderblock prison receded, Ripper felt like the wind. her ears were back and her body moved in one long stretching graceful rhythm. Ripper's tongue lolled out, bringing to her face a dog smile, with angry shouts getting fainter and fainter and Ripper ran and ran. Right. Then left. Then right down Burnt Mill Road.

For the next ten months, Ripper ran with a pack of wild dogs around Burnt Mill Road. While Ripper was not the leader, she more than held her own in the pack. The leader was a Doberman named Rusty who jumped his fence one day and never found his way back home. He was dumb but brave and had killed a rattlesnake that Ripper had accidentally shit on. The pack of dogs was legendary around Burnt Mill Road and many sightings were reported. They were stalked and shot at a time or two. They lost a wiener dog named Junior when a teenage boy tried his father's .22 for the first time.

Tammy would hear intermittent reports from people she knew that Ripper was running wild on Burnt Mill Road, but she also heard that the dog kennel had sold Ripper to a vet school where she was vivisected. She knew how these things worked. It was only when Roy's oil field buddy Cleat told them he saw Ripper that Tammy actually let herself believe Ripper was running wild. So, one

Saturday Tammy and Roy went out to Burnt Mill Road with a bag of Snausages and called Ripper's name over and over.

Ripper heard her name being called. She recognized the voice calling her, dimly remembering some other time, some other life. Or not. The pull was strong, but Ripper had grown to like running wild with the rest of the pack. Ripper stood between two worlds, but as Tammy's voice persisted and the other dogs got spooked and began to run away, Ripper was inclined to join them. Then she heard a familiar sound, a sound so pleasurable that her body shivered. It was the sound of a bag of Snausages being shaken.

Thus, ended Rippers pack running days.

Tammy settled down with Roy and they had a baby when Ripper was eight. Ripper did not like sharing the spotlight and growled ominously whenever Tammy held the baby. Remembering the fate of the kittens, Tammy packed Ripper off to her mother and brother Steve, just in time for his discharge from the army.

Steve Latino had dug down far enough in the flower bed next to the wooden fence. He hated Ripper even more now that he had to work so hard to bury her. Finished digging, he picked up the carcass and flung it into the hole he had just dug. As Ripper's body hit the ground, a Quarter came flying up out of her open mouth, hitting Steve Latino right in the face. He bent over and picked up the Quarter and put it in his pocket.

Steve felt little nostalgia for Ripper, but then again, he was not a sentimental person by nature. He always considered himself alone, against the world and he had no real true friends. He would have been very surprised indeed to know that Ripper had loved him best of all the people she had ever known and had been content to spend the final year of her life dodging his reckless slaps and feckless snubs.

May 1975-November 1975

The Quarter was used to buy a newspaper in Augusta Georgia. The headline that day was "SS Mayaguez seized by Khmer Rouge Forces." Farther down the page a headline read, "Man Kills Cow with Baseball."

The Quarter was used by William Beet to buy a guitar pick in Valdosta, Georgia. It was a tortoise shell pick that said "Fender. Heavy" on it. The pick was lost inside the sound hole of the guitar later that day.

The Quarter was given in change and used by Jerry Punt to buy a pack of Chuckles candy in Hanker, Tennessee.

The Quarter was given in change and used by Ileana Gouje to buy a feminine hygiene product in the ladies' bathroom at the Doople Diner just outside of Nashville, Tennessee.

The Quarter was given in change and used by eleven-year-old Billy Moldavian in the Nashville suburb of Hinton to fill up his dad's gas can for the lawn mower.

The Quarter was given in change to Mason Watt who lost it while taking out his keys to unlock his car.

November 1975
Nashville, TENNESSEE

That night, with the lights reflecting off the wet street making everything sparkle, Jim Groves found a Quarter in the gutter. He bent down and picked it up, carefully examining it for any miniature cameras or tiny transmitters. Satisfied that it was genuine, he put it in his foil lined pocket, where it would be safe.

Jim Groves was one of the many schizophrenic men who wandered downtown Nashville in a daze, furiously smoking cigarettes and thinking out loud, awash in a world that was not only terrifying but also unreal. What Jim thought about while wandering was cosmic and religious and connected and important and scary and beautiful and awesome and crushing and his attempts to explain it to other people had resulted in his being locked up and narcotized several times.

Twenty years ago, he had been a brilliant graduate student who forsook a research job on a history of King George II for teaching. One day, while student teaching, he heard someone say in his ear that Jesus was outside in a limo and wanted to talk to him. Jim went outside where sure enough, there was Jesus, in a spangled jumpsuit that glittered with ten thousand rhinestones. Jesus told Jim that he was happy about the way the earth curved so smoothly and that Jim had better shape up or bad things would happen.

It was all downhill from there. Jim took a lot of acid around this time, hoping to get back with Jesus, because he had about a million questions to ask him. Such as, do you brush your teeth up and down or side to side? What is the proper way to show displeasure? Arms folded across the chest or hands on hips? Jim had to know these things. Inside their answers were elegant stratagems for getting through life. These were questions only Jesus could answer and Jim hoped every day that his taking acid would bring him closer. But it didn't.

Jim became eloquently inarticulate and spent six long years in the Tennessee State Hospital for the Insane, being sedated, electro shocked, bio feedbacked, water treated, sensory deprived, and therapied. When state funding ran out for the less severely impaired, he found himself on the streets of Nashville, which teemed with robots and surveillance cameras designed to get at Jim's most inner knowledge. That knowledge, which everyone was after, was the fact that the moon was actually a skull of the Lithic God Bezel as foretold in the Necromiconian. Jim had read all about it in the library.

Jim came to feel himself divine and because of this divinity he knew that he was being closely watched. It was to his credit that he learned to live with this omniscient surveillance and to deal, however furtively, with those he had to deal with. In his day-to-day dealings he pretended to be invisible so he could walk among them. when he went to the Loaf and Jug to buy beer and cigarettes, he made sure to act like all the others, to keep his head down, to not engage the eye cameras which could read his retinas.

Often, he would strike up conversations with the robots and androids who stared at him on the street. He would let them know in oh so subtle ways that they weren't fooling him at all. He was considerate and fearful all at once and he reached out to the robots, as if they could take mercy on him if they knew how scared he really was.

"Do you know where the boot is?"

"Pardon me?"
"Pardon. The boot. Like John Wilkes Booth a long boot that goes up to the thigh. Sensual pleasures are an illusion. I know robot mind. I know the reflective emotions of silicon. Are you a priest?"

"Ah...no.."

"I believe in God. I know of God. His limousine is white and has to be reinforced to bear the weight of his golden robes."

"Uh uh."

"He tells me to use the sink not the bath tub. The tub drains straight to hell. Sometimes I hear the screams when I put my ear to the drain. Like that song. You know. The song about drains. Are you a priest? I need to confess father."

"Uh, would you excuse me?"

Jim roamed downtown in a bold display of courage. He would walk tall right among them and dare them to lock him up again in one of the many concentration camps in the Midwest. Through it all Jim read his bible, huffed gas while smoking cigarettes and spoke with Jesus and monitored those who monitored him. Often, he would struggle to uncloud his mind. The robots had the power to shift your thinking, which is what made him schizophrenic. They used magnets or something. But the joke was on them. *I am not schizophrenic,* Jim repeated to himself like a mantra.

I am not schizophrenic. I am wide awake. I am wide awake. I'm not sleeping.

After pocketing the Quarter, he had found, Jim made his way to Burger King where he liked to drink their coffee and watch the little android surveillance Koi fish swim about in the water. These machines were the most realistic, Jim decided and he would like to take one apart some time to see what kind of technology they employed.

Their bulging eye cameras obviously shot in 3-D. Jim looked around to make sure no police were watching him. He looked down into the Burger King fountain, with its cool rushing sound of gurgling water softly bubbling, making the water sparkle like lights reflected on a wet street.

The huge orange fish swam near the surface, looking at Jim with their bulging eyes, hoping he would throw them the remnants of a Whopper or two. Instead, Jim plunged his arm into the cold water and pulled out the heftiest fish.

This fish, startled, panicking at this sudden change of dimension, gasped and twisted in Jim's hand. Jim stuffed it in his backpack and quickly walked to the back alley behind Ghent Ford. The back pack squirmed in his arms, a sensation that revolted him.

In the alley he withdrew the thrashing, gasping android and laid it on its back. Its pitiful lashings began to cloud his mind and it took a supreme effort of will not to succumb to pity and release it. Instead, he took his sharp Swiss Army knife and cut into its soft belly, immediately inserting his fingers, probing for diodes and levers and batteries.

The mind clouding thrashing had succeeded and his mind was tricked into thinking he was holding a handful of pulsating fish guts when he knew that it was really some sort of bioengineered hydraulics. He had learned long ago never to trust his physical sensations. He knew the guts were only an illusion, an evasion of the Real Truth.

Jim saved the guts and plucked out the 3-D camera eyes for later examinations in the privacy of his home, a furniture-less apartment full of shredded documents he had gotten from the Mental Health Clinic dumpster, empty cans of gasoline and piles of cigarette butts.

The fish had stopped thrashing now and Jim picked it up and carefully brought it back to the Burger King Fountain, where he dropped it back into the water. He turned to leave but stopped, remembering something. He withdrew the Quarter he had found that morning in the gutter and threw it into the fountain with the rest of the robot fish. He threw it in the fountain to be with the rest of the coins there.

 For luck.

March 1976
<u>Jefferson City, MISSOURI</u>

"We gotta find a way to get high!"

"Shh! My parents will hear you Tommy! They're bed is right above us."

"I'm dying!"

"I know."

"God, I wish we had some beer."

"I know man. I'm dying."

Richard and his friend Tommy dug around through the mess that was Richard's basement bedroom. It was a typical teenager's bedroom in that is resembled the scene of an earthquake, or a mass murder. It was late, and Richard and Tommy had just finished watching "The Great Race" on Channel 7's Midnight Movie. Now they desperately rooted through the piles of dirty clothes and junk, looking for anything that would get them off. Tommy came across a large economy size can of aerosol spray deodorant.

"Hey check this out!"

"So what?"

"It can get you high!"

"Fuck you man. That can't get you high."

"Todd Minerich said that the spray stuff can give you a hellacious buzz. I'm going to do it."

"I ain't going to do that."

"Well, I am. I'm gonna get high. I'm dying!"

Tommy took one of Richard's dirty socks and rolled it up into a ball. Then he sprayed the sock until it was soaked with the antiperspirant. He jammed the dripping sock into his face, inhaling deeply; as deeply as is humanly possible. meanwhile Richard was reading the can intently.

"Tommy! This says CAN BE HARMFUL OR FATAL IF INHALED OR SWALLOWED! You just did both!"

Tommy lowered the sock from his red face, his eyes glazed and unfocused. He took in what Richard had just said and the redness in his cheeks disappeared. A bolt of fear ran down Tommy's back. They could hear Richard's dad snoring loudly in the room above them. They spoke in low and solemn tones.

"Fatal if inhaled man."

Tommy sat there with the sock halfway between his face and the floor. His eyes were still unknowing and confused.

"Oh fuck..." he whispered.

Currents of blind terror were coursing through both of them. Richard looked at Tommy as if he would drop dead any second. Tommy too, feared imminent heart failure, cringing at the thought of the hammer blow to come. So, they sat, silent, staring. Then the moment passed.

"You gotta drink some milk." Richard said finally. "It's like poison. They make you drink milk."

Tommy nodded, still too grief stricken to utter a word. They went into the filthy, cluttered kitchen, where they opened a crusty fridge and took out a plastic jug of yellowish milk. Tommy took a greedy swig then retched.

"It's sour!"

"You gotta drink it anyway! You might die!"

The urgency in Richard's voice triggered the fear jolt in both of them and Tommy took another huge swallow of the thick milk.

"I'm gonna puke..."

"No! If you puke you might die! Your guts might come up! You can't puke!"

Tommy looked at Richard, his eyes filling with tears. They waited. Tommy kept the milk down. His head was getting light and the fear was making him dizzy.

"Richard, I think my brain is shutting down. I'm dizzy..."

Suddenly Tommy wheeled and vomited into the sink. Richard tried to quiet him so his parents wouldn't wake up, but Tommy wasn't concerned with that right now. he was sure that he was vomiting up all of his guts, instead of the cherry Slurpee and rancid milk he had drank

"Oh my God! " Richard said when he saw the foamy bright red vomit. He hustled Tommy back down into the basement, his mind screaming all the time. Tommy seemed dazed and was trembling like a scared dog. They sat down on the bean bag chairs in Richard's bedroom. They turned down the lights and put on a Harry Chapin album. They didn't know what else to do. They sat, listening to the quiet music punctuated by the faint syncopated snoring of Richard's father coming from the vent.

"How do you feel now?

"Kind of queasy."

Tommy had settled into an infinite sadness. he was resigned to his fate. He was going to die. They'd all be sorry now. Richard thought about how he would tell Tommy's parents. What would he say? That he just woke up and found him dead? Was there a way they could trace the poison to his antiperspirant can? He knew he had to throw the can way. Destroy the evidence. He began to hate Tommy for leaving him in such a mess. Sure, he gets to die, but Richard's left holding the bag. What an asshole.

"You can't die here."

"What?"

"You can't die here. I'll get into trouble. You have to go outside and die in the backyard. Or go to the park and die there. Not here. I have to sleep here you know."

Tommy started to cry. It was all so sad. So sad. He was young. He hadn't even gotten close to getting his dream of becoming a gentleman lyricist off the ground. And now it would all be over. And his best friend, his best friend, was abandoning him. It really was true.

 You die alone.

"Your only chance is if you can stay awake and stave off the coma." Richard said authoritatively referencing all the medical shows he had ever been forced to watch with his father. Tommy's tears had unnerved him. The best way to deal with them was not to notice. That was always the best way.

"I don't want to die! I don't want to die! Tommy cried, appealing to God. Richard felt the shock of true fear and embarrassment. He just wanted to turn back the clock. Anything to go back. Please.

"Okay," said Tommy, pulling himself together. They faced each other, each trying to keep the other awake. But as the minutes passed a sense of resignation crept in. Richard was getting tired of waiting for Tommy to die. It had already been an hour. He wished he would just get on with it. Why did he have to hold so tenaciously to life?

Tommy too, was getting impatient. He was starting to like the idea of dying. He envisioned his funeral with Lisa Huser crying over his grave, sorry that she had treated him so badly. He would achieve teenage immortality and would get a full-page photo in the yearbook.

"I can't make it. I'm falling asleep."

"That's not sleep that's a coma Tommy!"

"I know. But I can't do it. I just can't."

"Yeah. There's nothing else we can really do."

"I'll go out on the backyard if you want me to."

The room fell silent. Even the snoring had stopped.

"No. Stay here."

"Thanks."

Again, the silence was as dark as the night. Richard took one last look at his friend and turned off the bedside lamp.

"Richard?"

"Yeah?"

"I'm sorry."

"It's okay. (Pause) is there...is there..."

"What?"

"You know, is there anything I need to...tell people? Anything you want me to say tomorrow?"

Tears sprang to Tommy's eyes. This was really happening.

"Tell them I...I...look I want to leave you my albums and that watch my grandma gave me, the one we broke with the hammer. And you can have my money..." He dug into his pocket but all he had was a Quarter. He passed it to Richard in the dark.

Richard felt the Quarter in his hand. It was warm and smooth.

Tommy floated off, his throat constricted from grief and fear. He would never see the sun again, never see a TV again, but he was ready. Already he could hear people crying at his funeral. And that made him fall asleep with a smile on his face.

Richard felt hopeless and braced himself to waking up with a dead body in the morning. In the dark, with his father's dull snoring a rhythmic background, he strained to hear Tommy's breathing, which slightly followed his father's until they seemed to form a third sound, an echo, that went onto include his own breathing. As he felt himself falling into sleep amid the chorus of sonorous breaths surrounding him, Richard let the Quarter drop from his hand onto the floor.

It was five hours until morning.

November 1976
<u>Memphis, TENNESSEE</u>

It was the week of Thanksgiving when Jerry Lee got the idea that Elvis might want to see him. In fact, it was the best idea Jerry Lee had had since he started drinking Jim Beam whiskey the day before. Or was it the day before that. Who the hell cared? Elvis wanted to see him. He called, didn't he? Or did he. Jerry Lee knew he talked to some damn person on the damn phone. Fuck it, Jerry Lee knew Elvis was still a good old boy at heart and those goddamn leeches that surrounded him were good old boys too. Jerry Lee knew how to handle the likes of them.

He had an elegant pistol that he wanted to give to Elvis, his old friend from the good old days, drinking mash liquor out behind the Sun Records studio, sipping it from a paper bag with the heat boiling off the pavement and the ripe smell of goat's head sticker plants and diesel fuel hanging in a miasma all around the town. The smells of a Memphis summer.

The pistol was a shiny nickel-plated Smith and Wesson with onyx grips. Jerry Lee forgot how he came into its possession, or even if it was loaded, although he assumed it was. It wasn't no goddamn good to him if it wasn't. Jerry Lee shouted through the gates.

"Goddamn you! You goddamn mama's boy!" He chortled with laughter. "Open up Elvis. I got your pistol! Goddamn you!"

Jerry Lee's famous voice was drowned out by the sparse traffic on Elvis Presley Blvd. Jerry could make out an ancient figure in an ill-fitting uniform, sitting hunched in a golf cart, staring at him.

"Fuck you, you goddamn hillbilly!" Jerry Lee shouted, waving the pistol in the air. "Fuck all y'all!"

When the police car showed up, it's blue and red lights were strobing, making Jerry Lee's eyes hurt. Graceland was brilliantly lit, as usual, and Jerry Lee knew Elvis was still up, probably watching TV. Elvis was a vampire, everyone knew that. Jerry Lee's bottle was almost empty too, but he knew he could get a fresh one from Vernon when Elvis wasn't looking too closely. Fuck it! Where the fuck is that damn hillbilly?

"Elvis! Git on out here! I got something for ya!"

Jerry Lee mashed the intercom at the wrought iron gates with musical notes on them. The guard who had been hiding in the shadows, Elvis's Uncle Vester, shifted uneasily in his golf cart, safely out of reach. He knew Jerry Lee from the old days, but he could also see that Jerry Lee was piss drunk and he wanted nothing to do with that.

Vester favored Jerry Lee's cousin Jimmy Swaggart, who was a humble man of God. Vester had called the police and there they were so Vester opened the little bible he always carried to get to him through the cool autumn nights, and started to read him some more proverbs.

Meantime, the Memphis police, who had pulled up with their blue and red lights strobing saw a disheveled middle-aged man clad only in a leather vest and pants, in the November night air. He had a whisky bottle in one and a pistol in the other and he was trying to climb over the iron fence.

Officer Glenn Procrustin and his partner Officer Rufe Wains, drew their pistols and ordered the man to get down off the gate. Right now.

"Goddamnit!" The man swore at them. "Elvis called me up and tole me to come right on over here. I come to bring him this here pistol and to talk some things over with him. Goddamnit!"

"Put the gun down now sir!" Officer Wains shouted; his heart pumping so fast that its roar flooded his ears.

"I'm gonna get in one way or the other!" Jerry Lee roared, but when he saw the fear on the officer's faces his immediately surrendered the gun. He may be a drunken fool, but he knew better than to mess with pistols when nervous young kids were pointing guns at you.

"Don't you boys know who I am?" Jerry Lee's voice was now silky, knowing.

"Please turn around and face the highway sir."

Vester, cautiously pulled up in his golf cart. Jerry Lee saw him and started hollering again.

"You tell that sonofabitch that if he wants to talk to me, he can damn well come and see me! Fuck him and fuck all y'all!" Jerry Lee spat at Vester, as the officers took his whisky bottle away. In one smooth motion, before the officers could even react, Jerry Lee reached into his vest pocket and withdrew a handful of change, flinging it through the gate at Vester. The coins jingled on Graceland's driveway and the Police stuffed a grunting, growling Jerry Lee into the back of their car. They nodded at Vester, who nodded back, then used the blue and red flashing light to examine the coins on the ground.

He saw a Quarter and some pennies, so he picked up the Quarter, putting it in his pocket, and as he watched the police car drive away, he kicked the pennies off to the side with the rest of the offerings and got back into his golf cart which hummed back into the safe cocoon of darkness.

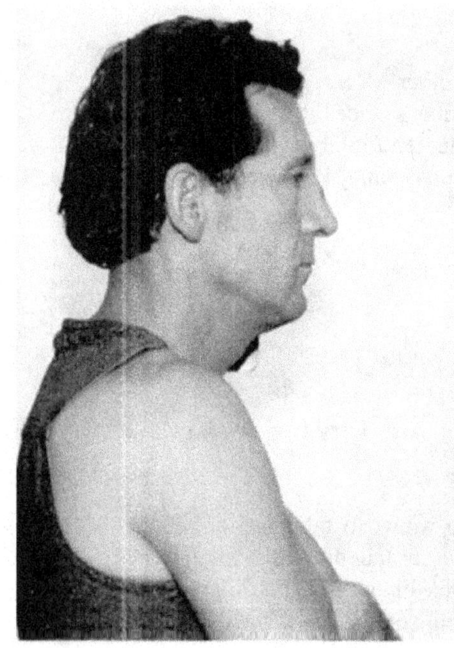
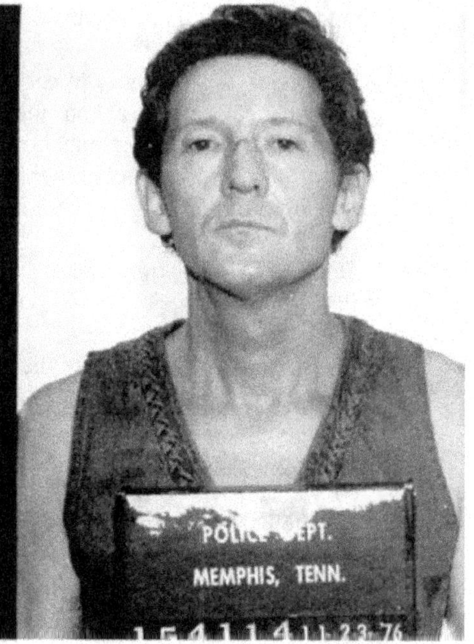

February 1977
<u>Manda, MISSISSIPPI</u>

It was a long way through the leaves to Richard Hossfield's grave, but Retta knew the way. She hadn't been there since 1963 when she and Earl came out from California to see his cousins and visit Richard's grave. That was when they saw the coin. It was placed exactly in the center of the "o" in Richard's last name. Just a coin, a nickel some joker put there. But somehow it irked Earl terribly and he snatched it away and threw it toward one of the other graves. He would never talk about it.

Now Retta came out alone and could see that the grave was overgrown and the empty flower pot was chipped and full of dead leaves. The coffee in her stomach sloshed like waves on a beach and she had to steady herself. It was all so long ago and Richard had been gone for so long she often wondered if he wasn't just a figment of her imagination all along. But no, here was his grave. And beneath this dirt and dead grass was her boy.

 Her little boy.

The man in the office told her the plots weren't selling very well and Retta was disappointed. They had bought their plots when Richard died in 1938, each on one side of him, but Earl was buried in San Diego, alongside of the golf course he loved so much, where there were no trees to obscure the view to the ocean.

Retta too, had lost all her ties to Mississippi; except for Richard's grave. She looked at the tree that had grown up beside the grave. She imagined the roots entwining Richard's little white casket, like strong arms, cradling it. This tree was Richard. It had been fed by his body. His shell had been absorbed into it and when she touched it, she could feel warmth. And life.

The cemetery had grown and sprawled since her last visit and now Richard's grave was near a fence, the other side if which had people raking and picking at the dirt field. Retta was surprised to find herself violated by their presence, not that they were paying any attention to her. She didn't know what to think or feel. But Richard wouldn't know the difference. He was dead and he'd died a long time ago. He died in her arms. He died with a smile on his face.

Richard's grave was near the stone doll house, which marked the grave of a little rich girl who was killed by a drunk truck driver. A sparrow had built a nest in its concrete gables and sang out a warning as Retta turned her head toward it. A distant *Tatatatatatat* from a woodpecker with a sharp white bill echoed in answer and a small fragrant gust of wind made the dead winter trees rustle like a giant woman's dress. It blew a delicious brew of scents; pine and dirt and weeds and distant rain.

Richard had died in the winter.

As she cleared away the weeds from his headstone, revealing his name, so seemingly permanent carved into marble, she saw a glint of silver and uncovered a Quarter covering the "o" in his last name, just like the last time. She picked it up and examined it. It was an old Quarter. It wasn't tarnished too badly. It didn't look like it had been there too long. She wondered whoever could be doing this to Richard, never thinking that it might be a tribute or maybe nothing more than a coincidence.

She started intently at her son's name, catching herself from falling, gazing steadily at the marble headstone that had cost her and Earl $114 in the middle of the depression. All she could remember was the argument they had that day. She didn't know if it was sunny or cloudy.

Retta rubbed the Quarter between her fingers and sniffed but could not bring up another tear for Richard. He'd be a middle-aged man now with an entire life already behind him. Retta didn't know why she dwelled on such things. She had come here to sell her plot and say goodbye.

Goodbye.

Tatatatatatat.

 The white billed-woodpecker answered from farther away. Another gust of wind.

Retta's grief for Richard had long ago ceased to be real, but the pain lingered out of habit. If only he hadn't picked that scab. They could have saved him from the blood poisoning two years later. They had a drug then. "Richard if you pick that scab you could get blood poisoning and die." Sometimes it was hard to believe he had ever lived.

"Mama...I'm going high high...into the sky..."

That is what Richard said in his delirium as the blood poisoning spread through his brain. Then like an empty hand puppet he was gone. Just gone and it was over. She wished she could remember everything he had said so she could convince herself that he had really been alive and living on this earth. But all she could hear in her memory was, "...I'm going high high...into the sky..."

Under her feet was a constellation of dead leaves. Richard was everywhere.

A bird singing in a voice she was hearing for the first time.

Tatatatatatat. A faint and far away answer.

A woman's dress rustling.

Just the hint of a distant fire.

In her hand, silver.

February 1977-January 1978

The Quarter was spent by Retta Hossfield at Woolworth in Bankle, Mississippi. It was given in change to Mario Lengration, who ate lunch at Woolworths every day. He always ordered the same thing. Grilled cheese sandwich, vegetable soup and a Coke.

The Quarter spent almost a year in the jar of Mario Lengration, a HVAC technician in Hurl, Mississippi. It nestled among pennies, nickels, dimes and other quarters until a mid-winter's night poker game when Mario lost it to Mennen Ingram who used it a day later to buy a pack of gum.

The Quarter was given in change to Herk Mank, a truck driver who was hauling nuclear waste to Florida, where it was to be dumped into the ocean.

The Quarter was spent on a condom in the truck stop restroom in Skakle beach, Florida. It was collected from the machine and stolen by the attendant, Willie Deel, who used it later that day to buy cigarettes.

The Quarter was given in change to Mike Bail, whose wife Betty later found it in the pocket of his pants while doing laundry.

March 1978
<u>Vero Beach, FLORIDA</u>

Betty withdrew the old metal box from her closet. She hadn't opened it in years. She had told the story often, but not lately, and it thrilled her to stand outside herself and think about her small bit part in History.

"See?" She said to her twelve-year-old granddaughter Reah. "Here it is." She opened the box, that looked like an old red tackle box with a buckle latch and a wire top handle, and withdrew some faded newspaper clippings and an old school notebook. Reah looked on disinterestedly.

"Was that yours?" She asked looking at the ceiling.

"Yes," said Betty, opening the book. "See?" She pointed to a column of girlish scrawls on a notebook page.

"Right here was when I first heard her. My father had built this shortwave radio and he had the largest antenna in this part of the country at that time... made it out of the frame of an old blimp."

"A blimp?" Reah laughed. The only blimps she knew were the Cloy sisters at school.

"Well, the blimp was just used to make my dad's antenna. It was these clippings I wanted to show you."

Reah looked at them with little interest. "They're old." She said, hoping it would be enough.

"Haven't you ever heard of her?" Betty asked, the feeling dawning on her that Reah had no idea what she was seeing.

"Well, I think I saw a movie once. Didn't she crash her plane?"

"No one knows," Betty said wistfully. "But I was the last person to ever hear her voice. On the shortwave my dad built. It was a freak harmonic. She was somewhere in the Pacific and here I was almost on the other side of the world."

"So, did they save her because of you?'

"No." Betty sighed. Maybe this wasn't such a great idea.

"So, did you used to get on that CB radio a lot then? What was your handle?"

"It wasn't a CB. It was a shortwave. You could listen to all kinds of things from all kinds of places. One time I even heard Japan. During the war."

"So, they never rescued her?" Reah asked looking at the faded picture of the woman in the old newspaper clipping. "Did she die?"

"I suppose so." Betty said sadly, remembering the voice, the frantic edge and the eerie static that made it all seem like a dream after all these years ago. She had just been a girl.

Reah studied the newspaper clipping. "Amateur Radio Enthusiast Hears Distress Cries of Amelia Earhart: Girl Ham Operator 12, Hears Aviatrix's last broadcast on shortwave. "Help us" Says Flier."

There was a tinkle of bells from outside.

"Grandma! Can I have a Quarter? It's the snow cone man!"

July 1978
<u>Lincoln, Illinois</u>

James Gotum always kept a roll of Quarters for his laundry and his poetry submissions.

James Gotum was proud to be a poet. He wrote good poetry and had the satisfaction of seeing most of it published in small, modest little zines which usually served only to aggrandize their makers. Yet, James had been admitted into their circles, not because of the quality of his poems, which were only okay, but because of the sheer volume of his submissions.

James prided himself on his methods and industry in the creation and marketing of his poems. Why, anything was liable to suggest a poem to him out of the blue, anything at all, and then he would be off. His trademark was brevity in his poetry because he knew damn well that if it came down to publishing long poems or a short poems, the short poems always won.

James was determined to see his work in print. This validation, while meaningless, was important to him on a level that not even he fully understood. He subscribed to Writer's Digest, researched his markets, tailoring his poems to fit each one just so. Every year James bought a copy of the Writer's and Poet's Market book. Sure, it was expensive but the poetry markets were volatile and James had to keep up to maintain his acceptance/submission quota.

 Increasingly though, he had started to perversely send poems that were the opposite of what Writer's and Poet's Market said a particular magazine wanted. For James, the challenge was becoming about trying to win them over. Who knew? James knew there was a market for everything.

He spent over fifty dollars a month on postage and supplies to send his poems out into the world. While James himself had never been farther than Springfield, his poems had traveled the world.

One he had the inspiration for a poem, James would carefully write it out with a fountain pen in a small black notebook. When he had down the feverish first draft, he would write a number in red ink at the top of the page. Then he would roll and expensive piece of twenty-four-pound bond paper into his IBM Correcting Selectric and carefully type out the final draft of his poem. James rarely made any real changes from the first to final drafts.

Once the poem was typed to his satisfaction, James would take care to sign it at the bottom and add his copyright notice at the bottom. When he had accumulated three such poems, he would ready himself for submission.

James never sent cover letters. He didn't believe in them. They were just a waste of his valuable time. He did enclose witty Xerox bios with the long, long list of credits to bring the editors to their knees. As soon as a market was chosen (more from vibes and mood than description and needs) he would type out the address in lower case, so his envelope would stand out.

Then would come the all-important SASE. That stands for self-addressed, stamped envelope. If you wanted any kind of response you needed to send in one of these with your poetry submission. To not do so was the sign of the rankest of amateurs. In addition to the all-important SASE, James liked to enclose a little gift, usually just a Quarter, to show his good will. It became like a superstition, and so that is why James kept a roll of Quarters on hand for his Laundry and his poetry submissions.

James had a ritual of always walking to a particular mail box which he considered to be lucky. He would slip his envelope into the mail box nonchalantly; saying a humble little prayer to himself and reflecting on the journey to come for his offerings, like little bobbing bottles in the waves, and James would listen for the dull clunk of the Quarter enclosed to insure his continuing Good Luck.

March 1979
Bismarck, NORTH DAKOTA

It was the very first day of Spring and Hud Weatherwax was thirsty. But then again Hud Weatherwax was always thirsty. Hud was a big brawny man with a terrible addiction that bothered him. Every single day of his life, Hud drank at least twenty Pepsi Colas. He was so addicted to it, that he sometimes woke up in the middle of the night, parched and bleary, making his way to the fridge and popping open a frosty red, white and blue Pepsi and draining it on one huge gaseous gulp. His throat would burn and when he returned to his warm bed, he'd still be thirsty and have terrible indigestion from the carbonation.

Everyone knew that Hud liked his Pepsi, but he felt that within himself that it was more than just liking pop. It was a goddamn monkey in his back. He needed it. There was a sense of shame about it that other people didn't seem to have when they sipped their Pepsi's. Hud always gulped his down, as if it were hot lava moving slowly down his parched gullet. The more he drank the more he wanted.

Sometimes Hud drank his Pepsi's in secret, often buying a couple twelve packs on his way home from the foundry, behind his wife

Tina's back. She nagged him about the sugar and how it was making him fat and his teeth brown and stumpy, but she had no idea how much he really drank. She would see him with a can and think it was the same can she saw him with five minutes ago. But it wasn't. Hud himself had stopped keeping track. Why bother? It only made him feel bad. Everything conspired against him. The chips were always salty.

The Pepsi commercials made him want to drink it. They showed Pepsi at its chilled and icy best; always in a sweating glass bottle surrounded by smiles. Even the Pepsi machine at work gave away free Pepsi's if you knew just right where to hit it. No man was that strong. Hud was a hopeless case.

Hud's moment of clarity happened late at night, while in the act of self-pleasure, watching a fresh and lively Pepsi commercial on TV, Hud suddenly realized that he was not responsible for his sickness. Hud was not a bad man who craved sweet water, but a victim, a tragic victim of corporate greed. He saw it all so clearly now. They *made* him drink it. They put chemicals in it so you *craved* it. It dried up your salivary glands and made you constantly thirst for more.

This train of thought staggered Hud just at the moment a Law Trackers commercial came on TV. A mob of smartly suited lawyers shuffled on a gray soundstage looking serious and competent, ready to get you your check ASAP! By the end of that week, Hud had made a deal with Alvin Bowen Attorney at Law to sue the Pepsi corporation for eleven hundred million dollars.

The newspaper carried a story about Hud's plight and addiction. He was briefly hospitalized for tests and then entered into a 12 Step program. Everybody was asking him what he was going to do with the money.

"Buy me an octopus." He replied truthfully, even though everyone thought he was being ironic and making some kind of metaphor for monopolistic corporate greed or something. But this was no joke to Hud. He planned to use the octopus in a tableau that he had in mind since he was a boy.

He would buy a huge fifty-thousand-gallon aquarium and fill it with sea water and neon colored gravel and a bubbling treasure chest with a skeleton pirate standing beside it to mimic exactly a cross section of the vast, deep ocean. then we would fill it with tiny ships and galleons and release his octopus to destroy them, like in a movie he had seen when he was a boy. He also had a plan for the octopus to fight a dolphin to the death, but that was for another time.

When he told Alvin Bowen Attorney at Law his plan for the money, the lawyer didn't blink, but immediately asked for a check for a hundred dollars as a "retainer fee." Hud pulled out a jar of coins and handed it over. Alvin Bowen, Attorney at Law, made a face.

"Um I didn't have time to go to the bank or anything." Hud mumbled, his throat parched.

"That's quite all right." Alvin Bowen Attorney at Law replied professionally. "Now let's get down to some of these tests results. before we start can I get you anything? There's a soda machine outside." He reached into the jar and fished out a Quarter holding it out to Hud.

Hud stared at the Quarter in his lawyer's hand.

"I'll have a Pepsi." He said.

October 1979
<u>Baige, OREGON</u>

Diana Barela was working her station on the line, pasting labels on glow-in-the- dark Frisbees as they made their way to the boxing machine and then to the cello wrap machine. She was not involved in her work; it took no concentration to do the same thing over and over for eight hours. Her mind was roaming freely through the universe looking at things, turning the around and over like a child who has found an interesting rock. She did not notice her boss, Victor Bobian shyly enter the room.

Recently there had been something happening when they spoke, nothing solid, but just a vibe, a feeling a hint of a chance. He wasn't much to look at, being stout and balding but she had recently given up being choosy that way. She wouldn't call their conversations flirting, but they were more than the regular boss/employee communications. There were undertones of something powerful welling up, something she did not want to admit to but something she carefully followed never the less.

Too bad Jock, the weak minded nineteen-year-old boy who cleaned the scraps along the assembly line her always hovered in the background. Nervous about the boss's presence he would chatter away oblivious to the fragile ballet winding itself down between them.

This night Jock was nowhere to be found. Victor had slipped in unnoticed and he planned to get as much alone time talking to Diana as possible. He wasn't sure how he felt about her. But there was something going on. No denying it. She was definitely not his type; skinny with fake blonde hair and braces on her teeth; most unbecoming for a woman almost fifty. But she had the kindest eyes he had ever seen, and her face lit up when she smiled like she must have smiled on Christmas mornings when she was a little girl.

"Hi," Victor said slyly, fixing her with his patented crooked smile. She looked up dully from her labeling and broke into her own illuminating smile.

"Well, hi," she said warmly as the lines smooth hum suddenly went into the background. She was forced to watch the Frisbees and not Victor but she didn't want to seem detached. She looked up every so often and blasted him in the eyes with eager interest.

"How ARE you?" She stressed the middle word and tilted her head, each movement a carefully choreographed performance. He responded to it with his own little dance.

"Good good." He let the conviction less words hang like a miasma.

"I know," she said sympathetically. "This time of year."

"Yeah." He said.

"It's been a year for you too? How strange that it should have happened to both of us at this time of year."

"It seems fitting."

"Yeah, better than if it happened in the spring."

"You know," Victor said. "I love the fall. But every bad thing that's ever happened to me has happened in the fall. My father died in the fall. My mother died in the fall..."

"I know what you mean," Diana said but she really didn't.

"When is your final hearing?" Victor asked.
"Oh well, we're still in mediation. We have a lot of properties. It's been an experience. At first, we just threw everything from the past at each other. Stuff we had mostly forgotten came back with a vengeance. Now it's more civilized and we're trying to work through it. How about you?"

Victor lowered his eyes. "The final hearing is November 27. If I can get out of going I will. I don't care anymore. I don't want to go. I mean, I know I have to go. But I wouldn't if it was up to me."

"Yeah," Diana said without much conviction. "I know what you mean." But she didn't.

"You know though," Victor continued warming to his subject. "You know I really love living alone."

"I do too." She cut him off then looked at the floor, blushing. They were sending signals a little too eagerly.

"I mean," Victor continued. "It's really nice not to live to anyone's agenda but your own. "

"I know. I can sleep until ten if I want.
"
"Yeah. My time is my own."

"You can eat wherever you want to.

"It's kind of liberating in that way."

"Yeah, but I still get a little restless. Sometimes I just want to get out. At first, I didn't like it. I was scared at night. I would check to make sure the doors were locked about five times before I went to bed. I don't do that anymore. I got comfortable. But I still get restless."

"Funny you should say that." Victor mused. "I've been feeling that restlessness myself. I've been taking a lot of walks. I've locked myself into a really rigid routine and that's what's kept me on the rails. I get nervous if I miss my walk. Kind of boring alone though."

"I love walking."

"Have you ever walked in a neighborhood and just vibed off all the houses? I mean it's like as you walk by and look at them you get little glimpse of what Easter mornings were like or you get a snapshot of a summer day or you fell a Friday night sleepover..." Victor stopped himself because he sounded weird and he was revealing the deepest part of himself, something he never ordinarily did.

"No. That never happened to me." Diana answered, confused.
There was the slightest pause. A line had been crossed and both parties had leaped back as if afraid of a powerful jolt.

"So, how's it going for you? You know, emotionally and stuff."

"I'm okay with it." Diana said resolutely. "It's a shame but we were having troubles for a long time. We just couldn't admit it. It becomes a matter of the pain of change versus the pain of staying the same. You know?"

"Yeah. I'm, having trouble letting go. I mean it was different with me. I had no idea...no time to prepare. She said she knew a year before that she wanted out but I had no idea. She wouldn't even give it a chance. My son is heartbroken. It's hard. It's hard to adjust..."

"Yeah, we were together for a long time..."

"I bet I got you beat! 28 years!" Victor sounded proud of his accomplishment. Her face did not show her concern.
"Well, we had fifteen years. But he traveled a lot. I was alone. So, it wasn't as big of a shock as it could have been. Still, I'm living in one of our rentals now and it's pretty run down. I was used to a much nicer house and life..." Diana stopped herself because she could see her words reflected in Victor's facial expression.

"Letting go of it is hard for me. This summer my house was robbed. I lost things that I had for years. Decades. But you know what? I couldn't get mad. Hard as I tried it didn't make me mad. I kind of felt like I had been set free. Of course, I wouldn't have felt that way if I hadn't had insurance."

"Insurance is good." Diana agreed.

Another slight pause, this one indicating a dead spot had been reached. Both were appalled at the total lack of interests they had with one another.

"Did you get through that book? Victor asked referring to a copy of The Prophet by Kahil Gibran he had lent her.

"Well, you know I kind of took what I could from it. It has a lot of good ideas." She rolled her eyes, not knowing the devastating effect it had on Victor, who worshipped the book and its philosophy.

"Yeah." He was disappointed because it had changed his life and he hoped it would do the same for her.

There was a harsh silence that entered the room like a cold wind.

"Hey one of these days we should..."

Jock entered the large room a sound of a flushing toilet following him, swaggering and twirling his keys. The room seemed to change character. The lights grew brighter and another version of reality took over. Victor and Diana exchanged knowing wry smiles and Victor started to leave with Jock so he could begin his inspection. On his way out he saw something shiny lying on the floor, head's up.

Victor bent down and picked me up.

"Found a quarter!" Jock exclaimed, agog with jealousy. "Lucky guy!" Victor flipped the Quarter to Diana who caught it. Her hands were warm and moist.

"Here you go," Victor joked. "It's pure profit. Give someone a call. On me."

He looked at her meaningfully and thought she looked back, and then he went out the door with Jock.

November 1979-December 1980

The Quarter made its way east in a Brinks truck, deep inside a canvas bag full of other Quarters. There were mostly new Quarters in the bag, but there were also some old ones. A 1928S, worn and blackened, spoke of the depression and its time in the pocket of a soldier in Europe. A 1951D told of its decades beneath a soda machine in Muncie Indianan only to be found by a toddler who promptly swallowed it.

The Quarter was used as change at the First National Bank of Scranton, and used later that day in a cologne machine in the bathroom of a Shell Station just off the parkway.

The Quarter was used to purchase a soft drink in Upstate New York, a candy bar in Connecticut and six songs on a juke box in New Jersey.

The Quarter was placed on the edge of a planter in front of the Dakota Apartment building in New York City on the morning of December 9, 1980. It joined other coins, flowers, drawings and tribute, but was soon covered up by a fine layer of dusty snow.

The Quarter and most of the other coins left on the planter were collected by a homeless man named Wister, who used them to buy a small bottle of strawberry flavored vodka.

The Quarter once again headed west on an airplane, rolled tightly in a paper roil, squeezed between a 1961S and a 1979D.

The Quarter was given in change at the Dollar Store to Dan Horstmenst in Preston, Idaho.

January 1981
<u>Preston, IDAHO</u>

It had just started to snow when Dan walked out of the Safeway with some cayenne pepper for his wife. She was making chicken chili and while Dan hated any kind of chili that didn't contain hamburger, we went along because in his sixty years he had learned the hard way that getting along was better in the end.

As he emerged from Safeway the light of the day, the smell of the air, the snowflakes staring to flutter down, the stillness of the season touched something deep inside of him. Since his cancer came, he had experienced many such moments of unaccountable emotion; a deep and often humiliating episodes for a truck mechanic like him. Why even last night he had been embarrassed to have his wife see him weeping at an episode of "Little House on The Prairie."

The smell of snow in the air took him back forty years to his childhood on the western slope of Colorado, where on his father's onion farm, he had learned to use all his senses to tell the weather. He could tell now that this snow was nothing big, but it was pleasant, fat big flakes drifting slowly down from a white sky, the low clouds seeming to muffle all sound except for the tingling tinkle of the Humane Society volunteer.

Instinctively reaching into his pocket, Dan withdrew a Quarter and put it into the blue metal pot and was rewarded by a toothless smile from the bundled bell ringer. Dan stood, staring at the slit in the bucket where his Quarter had just gone. It reminded him of something he used to do the farm. His father had a blue metal trash drum that he used for several things. Dan remembered with a shudder of dread how he would take unwanted kittens to the drum, snap their necks and toss them in and then incinerate them.

At the time, it had not seemed that big of a deal. Dan was young and the practical harshness of farm life had hardened him to such matters. But now the kittens came back to him, their tiny pink mewling mouths and bright eyes so trusting. And now Dan knew he was going to go to hell for killing all those kittens.

And so, he wept.

"You okay mister?" The bell ringer asked him. Dan nodded and withdrew a ten-dollar bill, putting it into the slot of the blue metal bucket. The bell ringer nodded as if he knew everything and Dan moved out into the parking lot. His chest felt tight and the light had shifted, casting ominous afternoon shadows against the steel white sky.

April 1982
Pueblo, COLORADO

It was getting dark just a little later now. Curtis recognized that he had turned the corner on another season. The parking lot tonight at the library was especially dirty and windblown from the warm dusty Chinook winds coming off the Sangre De Cristo mountains.

Curtis was coming to meet Snuggy Latka to sell him a dime bag of pot. Curtis had been selling pot for over a year now and doing quite good at it too. Curtis had known Snuggy Latka since high school where he was famous not only for his inappropriate nickname but because he was an all-state wrestler with a penchant for hanging himself.

Snuggy wasn't shy to admit that he preferred self-love to the messy and confusing entanglements of women. "My hand never fucked some other guy," he'd say bitterly, making a masturbatory gesture and rolling his eyes like a monkey. His fondness for strangling himself started when he read an article about autoerotic asphyxiation. "It fucking feels good!" He enthused to all his startled friends. "Don't worry. See, I hold a Quarter in my hand. If the Quarter drops, I know it's time to ease up." Snuggy always carried a Quarter with him at all times. He would often show it to people.

Curtis found him where he knew he would be, sitting in the front seat of his white 1967 Impala with a twelve pack of Scotch Buy Beer. He was parked by the Goodwill store, a piece of parking lot perpetually in the shadow of the library and the Goodwill store, thus affording adequate cover. The rime of dirty snow and gray ice that formed there often lasted until June. Curtis got into the passenger side of Snuggy's Chevy. It smelled like beer and motor oil.

"Hey Snuggy."

Snuggy handed him a beer and chugged his own down. "Goddamn fucking metric system!" he blurted.

"Fuckin-A," Curtis said supportively. he tossed the baggie on the seat between them. "It's an eighth." Curtis said.

"How much in grams?" Snuggy hissed.

"Twenty bucks dude."

Snuggy dug in his pockets, pulling out wadded up dollar bills and fistfuls of change. He piled it all onto Curtis, knowing that in the dark car and awkward sitting posture, Curtis would have a hard time counting it. When he had exhausted his supply, Snuggy suddenly lunged at Curtis. "Hold up," he said, pawing through the coins in Curtis's outstretched hand. "Let me hang on to a Quarter." He chose one and instead of putting it in his pocket he clutched it in his hand.

Curtis drank deeply and tried to think of a way to leave. The thing he liked least about selling dime bags was the whole ritual of pseudo drug brother friendship that went into each sale. He had to pretend that he and Snuggy were friends and they would have to visit for a time so neither one of them felt weird that their entire relationship was based on weed.

Snuggy fumblingly loaded a charred and crusty wooden pipe, spilling pot all over the car.

"Don't you ever clean your weed?" Curtis asked, trying to sound amused.

Snuggy looked at him like he as crazy. "I can't afford to clean my weed dude. I paid for those seeds and stems. I'm supposed to throw them away?"

They passed the pipe silently. The car quickly filled up with spicy white pungent smoke.

"Want to hear my favorite joke?" Snuggy offered.

"Sure." Said Curtis. The beer was tasting better.

"Okay there's this guy see and he had a wife and a little kid and so forth..."

Snuggy sometimes used strange language. He had overheard someone tell his mother that he seemed to be very intelligent, so he took to salt and peppering his conversation with so forths, henceforths and be-that-as-it-mays. Warming to his story he began to talk faster, without taking any breaths.

"He grew up and shit and henceforth became a child of five ready to enroll in school. Then he goes to kindygardens and the guy the father says okay look you pull off all straight As and shit then you get anything you want. A puppy a TV anything. Any motherfucking thing you want. Okay so the kid goes on to make straight As and shit because it's fucking kindagardens so the dad is true to his word and so forth and he asks the kid what he wants and the kid says he wants a Pink Polka Dot Ping Pong Ball. The dad thinks okay the kid is five and he could have asked for a gold bar or some

shit so he gets him the Pink Polka Dot Ping Pong Ball. Okay then it's like first grade same fucking thing. The dad says you get straight As you can have anything you want and just like the year before the kid gets straight As. End of the year the dad asks him what he wants and it's the same thing. A Pink Polka Dot Ping Pong Ball. Okay be that as it may this continues on for the kids' whole school career. All through high school same fucking thing. Same deal same request. A Pink Polka Dot Ping Pong Pall. Okay and so forth. So now the kid is grown up and about to graduate from high school. The dad thinks okay now he's really gonna get me. He's gonna want a Corvette or some shit this time. But not the same thing. All he wants for graduation is a Pink Polka Dot Ping Pong Ball. The dad finally cracks. He says you have to tell me why you want this same fucking thing every year. A Pink Polka Dot Ping Pong Ball. The son laughs and says he'll explain everything to him later tonight but now he has to go to the prom. So, on the way to the prom the kid gets into a bad wreck on the highway his date is killed and the kid is in critical condition. He's not going to make it. So, the dad rushes to the hospital. He's at his son's side. The son is up to his last breath and the father begs him please son please tell me why why you always ever wanted a Pink Polka Dot Ping Pong Ball all those years. I have to know. The son smiles weakly and opens his mouth to tell him and then. He. Dies."

Snuggy took a triumphant hit off the pipe and stared out into the cool dark spring night. Curtis, dizzy and unfulfilled, watched the smoke rise from Snuggy's mouth like evil spirits.

"Here man, take this Quarter," Snuggy suddenly said, pressing the warm moist coin into Curtis's hand. "You never know." Snuggy added, enigmatically. Curtis opened the car door flooding the interior with light from the dome. He looked dubiously at the Quarter in his hand.

"Go ahead and take it," Snuggy said. "I don't need it."

Curtis got out and slammed the door, plunging the car back into its darkness. Curtis could see the cherry red coals burning in the bowl of the pipe as Snuggy took another hit.

"Hey!" Snuggy called after him. "Wasn't that the best fucking joke you ever heard?"

Curtis nodded but didn't really think so. Until later, when he decided that it really was.

January 1983
Clear Lake, IOWA

Re: How to Make An Ice House

Diane,

I'm very sorry to hear about Dewayne's sister.

When my mom was dying, she gave me a huge bottle of pills.

"Give them to me when I ask for them." She told me. It wasn't a request.

So, I hung on to this bottle of pills. When she was in the final stage, raving and ranting, out of her head, I asked her if she wanted her pills. She looked at me and said "Hunh? wha?" So, I tipped them down the loo, except for the valium.

Because of that valium I have no memory of her funeral.

But if she had looked me in the eye and demanded those pills, I would have given them to her.

Ah bad memories Diane. Sorry to hear it. Hope Dewayne will be okay. I am enclosing a Quarter in case you want to call.

Mike

February 1983-July 1984

The Quarter was not used by Diane to call her friend Mike as he hoped she would. Instead, she put the Quarter in her purse where it stayed for seven months, keeping company with half a pack of Certs; a lipstick without a lid, several feral coins and a wooden pen made by her dead Uncle John that didn't work anymore. She finally fished out the Quarter at a car wash one September afternoon and used it to buy a cotton candy scented air freshener.

The Quarter went from the change box at the car wash in Iowa to a change box in a huge industrial clothes dryer at the Lady Saver Laundromat in Oklahoma. It was used to dry several pairs of jeans worn by Clete Prout, who worked in the oil fields. He had to wash his jeans in Coca Cola to get the oil out of them.

The Quarter went from the coin box of a dryer in Oklahoma to the coin box of a peep show in the back room of an adult book store in Race, Nevada. The title of this particular loop was "A shot in the dark." It featured a young woman who enjoyed flicking the lights on and off as several suitors formed a ring around her and jacked off.

The Quarter went from the coin box of a peep show to the coin box of the Lutheran Trinity Church one Sunday in July, 1983. It was placed in the collection plate by Mansur Samuel, a shy farm boy who laughed when you punched him in the stomach. This novel reaction led to several brutal beatings leading to several operations later in life which ultimately led to his death twenty-nine years later.

The Quarter was deposited in the church account at the Oklahoma State Bank and Trust, where it was rolled and given in change to a young screenwriter, Kenny Pondel, who was buying at root beer Slurpee on a hot July day.

August 1984
<u>Montgomery, ALABAMA</u>

Kenny Pondel worked the graveyard shift at the Winston Hotel underground parking garage in downtown Montgomery. he sat all night in an aluminum and glass booth with a little portable battery TV, a cassette player and a selection of survival tunes. he sat all night in a glass and aluminum booth underground waiting for the next car to come and wondering if "She" would be in it.

"She" was his woman, his soul mate, who he had yet to locate on planet earth. Kenny pondered his life savings on the counter in front of him, in the harsh tube light of the parking garage. It was three in the morning and as usual it was time for him to search his soul. His life savings was just a fistful of change, mostly pennies and dimes and a single Quarter. Kenny pondered the Quarter. It was from 1963, a year he knew to be momentous. He wondered if it was a sign. Maybe his soul mate, maybe "she" was born in that year. That would make her twenty-one years old.

Perfect. Yes. It was indeed a sign.

At the tender age of thirty-three Kenny Pondel began to seriously wonder if he would ever find "Her." He felt as if he were constantly searching for someone, but he just didn't know who. He was certain he would know "her" when he saw "her." he was sure of that.

Kenny Pondel worked on a screenplay about his life. he had never written a screenplay before, but he attended the yearly Tulsa Film festival organized by the local Jaycees, and passed keen judgments on all the offerings. Kenny was a discriminate viewer of film and fancied himself somewhat of an expert on cinema symbolism.

Kenny Pondel saw his life as a movie that he was constantly directing, much like he did as a boy, when after watching the ABC Sunday Night Movie he would walk to school the next morning inside the face of the hero he had watched the night before. The movie of his life he saw now was a brooding noir which had steam venting from manhole covers and heavy overexposed moments of hand-held gritty realism.

The camera was always on in Kenny Pondel's mind. he would score his life movie with his favorite music, blasting it through headphones while his mind visualized the images to go with it. many times, this resulted in such moving Art that Kenny Pondel would break down in tears and sob and feel embarrassed about it afterwards, catching a glimpse of himself, red eyed and puffy, in the mirror while blowing his nose.

Kenny Pondel called his screenplay "The Interchange of Limits" which he thought was a fine ambiguous title worthy of literary respect from critics like himself. He'd been working on it for two years, alone in the parking lot booth under the harsh florescent light that buzzed like phantom whispers always right over his head.


```
                     "The        Interchange         of
Limits"
                A Play For The Screen By
                Kenneth  Tracy  Pondel
```

SCENE:(A parking lot booth. Night. The graveyard shift. Inside KENNETH TRACY PONDEL is working. He stops to reflect on a coin laying on the counter beside him. As he ponders it, we see it in close-up. It is a Quarter. KENNETH TRACY PONDEL ponders this Quarter for a moment, then places it back on the counter. He resumes his work, which is writing a screenplay called "the Interchange of Limits."

KENNETH TRACY PONDEL is a large but handsome man in his late twenties. He is handsome enough to overcome the effects of his thinning hair and his recent switch from glasses which he relied on to hide his face to contact lenses. He is also a master of judo and a fencing champion. KENNETH TRACY PONDEL has never been on a date. he's never kissed a girl. He's never held a girl's hand. The harder he tries to appear debonair the more retarded he seems. the tragedy is that he sees all of this clearly but is helpless to do much about it.

The parking garage booth is brightly lit but the garage that surrounds it is shrouded in gloom. KENNETH TRACY PONDEL is scribbling in a notebook while his little battery-operated TV is showing COSMOS narrated by the comforting voice of Carl Sagan.

            CARL SAGAN
            (On TV)
There is, we are told, an infinite hierarchy of universes, so that an elementary particle

in our universe would reveal itself to be
its own and entire enclosed universe...

(A car approaches. KENNETH TRACY PONDEL
looks up from his notebook.)

              CARL SAGAN
              (On TV)
...an infinite regression, universes within
universes endlessly. Our familiar universe
of galaxies and stars and planets and people
would be a single electron in the next
universe up, the first step of an infinite
progression...

(The car pulls up. It was a beautiful
WOMAN.)

         WOMAN
Excuse me handsome, but do you have a
Quarter I could borrow?

(KENNETH TRACY PONDEL picks up his lucky
Quarter and hands it to her without
hesitation. She smiles and laughs out loud.
KENNETH TRACY PONDEL laughs too and struck
by his sense of humor the WOMAN reaches out
and squeezes his hand. When he withdraws it,
he sees it has a hotel room key. The music
of COSMOS swells from the TV and the WOMAN
smiles and drives into the dark gloom of the
garage.)

Kenny Pondel never got any further that this in his screenplay
because his imagination couldn't come up with what would happen

next. When he got stuck like this, he would always turn to the telephone. His telephone was especially important to him because it was literally the only mode of communication he had with the outside world. Kenny liked the phone because he could be anonymous. He could be anyone he wanted to be and there was no harm done. He felt secure on the phone because no one was looking at him, they couldn't see the lumpy balding squinting man he had become. No one was judging him. He knew what he looked like. He knew that the image of himself he carried in his head movie was not how other people saw him.

This realization struck with full force on October 7, 1968, in high school gym class. he just suddenly got a glimpse of himself as others perceived him and it was devastating. From that point on Kenny Pondel was no longer so innocent, or hopeful.

Maybe this attitude was why females shied away from him. He remained untouched, uncaressed, unkissed by living words. Women seemed ill at ease around him. As if they feared he would leap on them and impregnate them with his mutant seed. They all looked at him with atavistic distaste.

Still Kenny Pondel had hope. Hope was his religion. It sprung eternal and perched without feathers upon his soul. He knew the odds. He had read somewhere that there were five women to every man on planet earth. Five! The odds were in his favor. He only had to be patient.

Kenny Pondel would always turn his little TV off at four. He would turn off the harsh blue white lights in the parking lot booth, lit only by the green button lights of the phone. His heart would stomp in his chest as he would dial the 800 number for the Party Talk Line. It wasn't phone sex, like his mother accused it of being. He had made the mistake of telling her how much this meant to him. Her declaration that he was a pervert wounded him because it was his way of reaching out into the world. What he did was pure. No one understood that.

He kept his Quarter ready just in case a beautiful woman drove up and asked if she could borrow it. The line rang and clicked and voices filled Kenny Pondel's head. Happy voices, sad voices, indifferent voices, everyone talking at once, nobody listened except Kenny Pondel.
The voices all reaching out from their blue rooms with their blue moves and no shadows, all equal in their need for contact. It was a perfect world on the phone filled with possibilities. Real people of his imagination talked to him, didn't judge him, didn't fear him.

They just talked.

 And Kenny Pondel listened. And as he listened, he saw the headlights of a car approaching.

September 11, 1985
Flint, MICHIGAN

The wind was blowing wet sheets of paper around like ghosts in downtown Flint. One page flew into Room 9 of the US MOTEL, a bottom of the barrel one step away from homelessness strip motel that abutted the post office and a block of projects.

Room 9 was occupied by Johnny Murchison, a sixty-nine-year-old man at the end of his rope. He had been drinking steadily all day, Yellowstone whiskey, guaranteed to give you a headache and now Johnny's head was pounding. He took some Nyquil to stop his head pounding, but then things got away from him.

It was all because of a Quarter. Johnny wanted to go out to the paper rack by the US MOTEL office and buy himself a paper. He wanted to read about Patton's advance into the forests of Germany and he wanted to know when he would be relieved. The taste of whiskey and Nyquil still in his mouth, Johnny couldn't get the Quarter into a slot made for a dime. So, he snapped.

He made himself a little nest directly in front of his open door; a barricade of scarred and broken furniture, his mattress and anything else he could pile up to hide behind. He moved his provisions into his safe zone. They consisted of a loaf of bread, four Pepsi's, the bottle of Yellowstone whiskey, and a can of Spaghetti-Os. He took stock of his ammo, one clip with sixteen rounds in it and another box of old ammo that he wasn't even sure would fire.

He started shooting, in an idle way, but his lack of serious ammunition meant he would soon be out of shells, so he began to take more care in his shots. His TV was on, a Lee Marvin movie. Lee Marvin was also shooting a rifle. Just like Johnny's.

"I'm here you sons a bitches!" Lee Marvin brayed on TV.

"I'm here you cocksuckers!" Johnny yelled, watching the muzzle flash from his rifle with a certain amount of impotent pride.

One of his bullets hit the frame house across the street. It struck a teenage girl named Missy who was doing the dishes. She had to go through seven months of physical therapy. One of his bullets went through the window of a gas station a quarter mile up the street. The hole it made in the drywall was pointed to with pride by the owners as being part of a notorious incident. One of his bullets ricocheted off the street and entered the wall of a house. The owners never knew how their picture of a sailboat on a moonlit lake got a hole in it. They briefly considered if they had ghosts.

Johnny could sense the growing interest in him outside, a rumble like the ocean, only in English. Then came a cacophony of sirens. Patton must be coming, Johnny thought in his addled brain. The Germans will kill me. I can hold out until Patton gets here.

On the TV was a newscaster talking excitedly about a sniper. Johnny felt good that he wasn't the only one. Someone else must have tried to buy a paper with a Quarter that wouldn't fit in a hole made for a dime.

The shots continued. One bullet ended up in the back of a passing pickup truck, harmlessly spent and laying docile in the bed to be found by the truck's owner much later and wondered about ever after. Another shot hit the cheek of the pioneer statue in Taylor Park, chipping the bronze and costing the taxpayer's $750 in repairs.

The Flint SWAT team emerged from a dark blue van driven at full speed from Frankenmuth, where they had been enjoying their yearly chicken dinner. They advanced slowly, cautiously as their training had prepared them to do. Officer Gary Smend, a third-year member of the elite was as jazzed as he had ever been. He brushed by the office of the US Motel; his machine gun raised to his shielded face. His heart was pounding, and as he looked around something flashed on the ground and caught his eye. A Quarter lay on the ground right by the newspaper rack. against all his training. Officer Smend reached down and picked up the Quarter, putting it in his vest pocket. He was seen doing this by his sergeant and was reprimanded a week later.

 In Room 9 of the US Motel, Johnny switched channels and tore off a hunk of bread from his loaf, chewing thickly and switching back and forth to see which channels were telling his story the best. He popped open a Pepsi and drank thirstily. The sugary burn felt good at the back of his parched throat.

He settled on Channel 9 Action News Flint's News leader and the anchorwoman Barb Butkovitch. She claimed Johnny had been shooting for two hours and that seven people were dead. That couldn't be. He'd only shot a few times. It had only been a few minutes.

One shot hit a police car, shattering the window.

One shot hit Kirk Higgin, 26 a printer's binder, in the head.

One shot a lawn mound in the yard of Eddie Caruso.

One shot tore through Angela Blaink's pancreas.

Now there was a commercial on Channel 9 Action News Flint's News leader and suddenly Room 9 was alive with tear gas, fire and noise. A high-pressure jet of water hit Johnny in the chest, a powerful fire hose blast that knocked the breath and the gun away from him. He didn't feel any of the shots that struck him in several places, nor did he hear the shouts or the spray. When the news came back on from the commercial, because of a fifteen second time delay, Johnny was somehow still firing, still alive somewhere in the air.

December 1985
<u>Detroit, MICHIGAN</u>

The guys at work liked to pick on Frank because he was a Mexican. At 61, he was way past his prime as a janitor at West High School, but he came to work every day, more or less, and little else was really required of him. The guys at work picked on Frank because he was a Mexican, because he was old, because he couldn't speak the language very well. He knew they all made fun of him, and it hurt his feelings but he was used to pain. Life was pain. Or at least Frank's life was.

He wasn't particularly smart, and after finding his wife in bed with another man he spent the next fifteen years trying to drink himself to death in revenge. This resulted not in a noble death, but a burst appendix in the drunk tank and seven thousand dollars in hospital bills. But Frank didn't drink anymore, he just accepted the hurt that went from the core of his bones through the heart of his soul. He accepted it and cherished it.

Frank was comfortable in his role as crew clown and he enjoyed the attention and downright affection it brought to him. He liked being one of the guys, even if it meant always being the butt. And Frank was an easy target. He wore the same clothes day after day, grimy and stiff and he reeked of body odor because he claimed water made his skin itch too much. It would get so bad that Bob, the head man, would have to tell him to take a bath, which elicited howls of protest from Frank.

"I Can't DO IT Bop!" He says, throwing his greasy baseball cap to the ground for emphasis. Paradoxically, Frank often wore several sets of rubber gloves while cleaning bathrooms to protect him from the "germans."

Frank's run was on the first floor of Ashton High, but he was mostly invisible to everyone there. On this day, Frank was standing inside the closet sized art display case in the main hall. He was swiping his dirty rag at the constellation of fingerprints that were smeared all over the glass. As the display was currently empty, people walking by were treated to the site of Frank, seemingly encased in a transparent cage. Students stopped and gaped, as if seeing him for the very first time.

Sensing his audience, Frank began to play along. Suddenly he started imitating a monkey; toothlessly grinning, hunching over and scraping his knuckle across the floor. It was an uncanny imitation, an almost preternatural transformation that left the hardcore students temporarily speechless. Then they erupted into shouts of mirth and confusion.

Mr. Harwich asked Bob if Frank was drinking again.

His run of the first floor of Central High was five classrooms and three bathrooms. Frank's favorite room to clean was Room 09, the Spanish room because he had a certain feeling for the teacher, Janna. She was a plump woman with black eyes and a small mouth and Frank loved her. He would always smile for her because it made her smile back at him. Frank liked to bask in the warmth of her insincere smiles.

As he went in shoving his janitor cart with its intrusive clatter, he heard music playing, Spanish music and saw Janna sitting at her desk, crying. The music was sad.

"This heart that still adores you
Is now dying
Afternoon by afternoon
Like the light at the end of the day.

Where are you? where are you?
Kill me heaven
swallow me earth
Take me Jesus If he doesn't come back"

"Hi Frank. Could you come back later?"

Frank headed out the door. He was sweating. He stood outside the classroom for a moment, listening to the sad music and the sound of Janna sobbing. The hallway was empty now, and the afternoon light had turned from gold to gray. Frank reached into his pocket and pulled out a Quarter. It was all he had to give her. He painfully bent over and placed the Quarter on the floor right in front of her door, right where she couldn't miss it.

He put it there for Janna, a treasure to cheer her up.

March 1987
<u>Windsor, ONTARIO</u>

"Show me."

"You show me first."

"No, you go first."

"No, I've already seen one. You go first."

"What did it look like then?"

"It looked like...an orange."

"An orange? You never saw one!"

"Okay then. Just show me yours. Then I'll show you mine."

"No, you go first, Then I'll think about it."

"Okay..."

"There. Are you satisfied?"

"It wasn't so much."

"Now you show me."

"No."

"But you promised! I showed you mine!"

"I'll do it for some money."

"All I have is a Quarter."

"Give it."

"But it's my last Quarter."

"Do you want to see it or not?"

"Well..."

"I guess you could go look at an orange instead."

"Okay. here."

"Wow."

November 1988
Moorhead MINNESOTA

The clouds came up fast over the lake.

Denny hurried to unlash the dead doe from the hood of his Ford. The brightness of the sky receded into graying shadow, as the water of the lake swelled, then released like a giant heartbeat.

"Daddy you know I didn't even want to come up here. I just thought we should make things clear, that's all. We both know what you did."

Denny silently hefted the dead deer over his shoulder, smearing his blue nylon windbreaker with thick black blood. Mandy followed her father into the large shed reluctantly. The quickly moving wind flipped her light hair into her mouth and she spat it out again and again.

As she watched his back sway under the weight of the deer, she was afraid of him all over again. Of his strange unresponsiveness. His clear-eyed sincerity.

"I just don't understand how you can be so unfeeling," she followed him into the shed. Denny said nothing, pretending Mandy wasn't there hectoring him, just like he used to do with her mother.

"She didn't just up and disappear daddy." Mandy turned and focused her gaze on the green gray undulating waters of the agitated lake.

"Mandy, I swear I don't know why you speak to me in such a way. I've never done anything to make you think such things about me. What your mother did was to hurt me and here you are blaming me and accusing me." They did not face each other but spoke facing outside, their words drifting into the chilling air and over the rolling lake.

"I want to believe you Daddy, but I know my mother did not just vanish into thin air. I know she wouldn't do that to me." Mandy felt her anger rise but her father's soft voice cut through it.

"Well, the question is would she do it to me."

Mandy again angered at his selfishness. "You might have fooled Kelvin into approving your new relationship, but don't expect it from me.

Denny patted the belly of the dead deer. "I don't need anyone's approval for Christy. I don't need anyone's approval for anything."

He rolled a metal barrel over and struggled to winch and hang the back legs of the deer onto chains, placing the head and front of the body over the barrel.

"What all have you got against Christy anyway. She likes you."

"She's younger than I am!" Mandy almost shouted. Denny didn't react. He started to skin the deer. He preferred to skin before gutting.

"I just don't see how you could forget her so fast. How you knew she wasn't coming back. How come there was blood..."

At the sound of the word, Denny peeled off the deer's skin. It took him seconds.

"What was I supposed to do? Wait for her to come back?" He grasped a large curved knife and plunged it into the doe's belly, pulling upward toward its throat. When he got to the throat, he had a vertical slash and thick blood started to drain into the barrel. The shed filled with an awful smell and Mandy used her scarf to cover her face.

"Christy loves me. " Denny said simply.

"I didn't come here to argue. We already went through all that in court. I..I..just..I just want.."

Denny turned to face her, for the first time his colorless grey eyes bored into hers, like ice cold lasers. She could see nothing in them but her own reflection. Mandy could smell the rain which had started falling on the far shore of the boiling lake.

"Your mother wasn't no saint." Denny said quietly, turning back with his knife to his deer. From the broken shed window, he could see the bright yellow light from the house and knew that Christy was there, waiting for him. Denny's eyes strayed to the dim full moon in the daytime sky high above the timberline of the mountain peak. The black slashing clouds quickly covered it, but Denny could still feel its heavy pull.

"Sean's waiting for me in the car." Mandy paused. "I used to really love this lake." She meant for it to hurt him but he showed no sign of it if it did. He knew Mandy was watching him. waiting. The blood on his windbreaker smelled like milk to him. It mingled with the heavy ozone rain smell that came into the room on the gust of wind.

Mandy walked down the gravel lane to her car where her husband Sean sat, watching the choppy waves. She got in and slammed the door, not looking at him. Sean started the car.

"Do you have the $1.25 for the toll?" She asked dully. Sean reached into several pockets and produced only a dollar.

"Great." Mandy said sarcastically, getting out and slamming the door. The rain was coming and the wind had picked up. She leaned back into the car.

"Keep the engine running."

She walked back toward the shed along the shore line of the lake and noticed how it mirrored the turbulence of the sky. She knelt and put her hand into the cold cold water and pulled out a bright round pebble worn smooth of billions of years of tectonic stresses and tensions.

She walked toward the shed, full of dread, it's dirty yellow light now switched on and a buzzing radio competing with the wind and now the thunder. In the doorway she saw her father with his knife, poised over a pink skinned body, upside down, legs splayed, blood draining into a big black plastic trash barrel. Denny turned and saw her, staring horrified, as if realizing something for the first time.

"I..I..do you have a Quarter I could borrow? For the toll?" She stammered, wanting only to leave to leave now.

Wordlessly Denny reached into his pocket and handed his daughter a Quarter. She accepted it without looking at him, and she rand all the way back to her husband.

"Ugh," He said as they drove away. "This Quarter has blood all over it."

"I know." Mandy said, watching the lake intently for the last time.

March 1987-December 1989

The Quarter was lost inside a couch by Randy Sternholm while he was losing his virginity to Nena Bridges. Their desperate fumbling on the couch in his parent's home in Pella, Iowa, produced not only a small baby nine months later, but years of misery for all parties involved.

The Quarter had rolled out of Randy's jean's pocket and the crucial moment and slid between the cushions of the couch, where it lay, inert and unknowing for over a year. It was dislodged while being vacuumed by Randy's mother Mary Lou, who was sick and tired of sitting on the couch and hearing the crunch of stale potato chips beneath the cushions.

The Quarter then rolled onto the floor beneath the couch, where it rested for many more months, privy to the rise and fall of insect civilizations all around it, indeed, even becoming the focus of a particularly nasty war between spider mites and tick fleas. This war lasted for over a month (seven decades in tick flea time) until the Quarter was finally won by the spider mites in a terrible battle of the inner spring batting. At the moment of ultimate triumph, the prize Quarter was found by Randy Sternholm himself and returned to his pocket for later use.

January 4, 1990
Pella, IOWA

Randy Sternholm reached into the coin jar, which had once held Gonzo's Sugar Pickles, and withdrew an old Quarter. If he won anything then it would become his lucky Quarter to be used in all subsequent scratch off games.

 Not that he was superstitious.

He had never bought a scratch ticket before. Had never even thought about it, but now that Iowa had the lottery, he thought he would give it a try. It's not that he was desperate for money, although he could use a windfall; a miracle to put his life Right. He wasn't destitute or needy, he was just a few thousand dollars away from having it all. It didn't seem like so much to ask at all. For a five-dollar ticket he could hope and dream to his heart's content. It seemed like a good trade to him.

The ticket was simple enough. Scratch off the silver coating and if you get three nutmegs, lightning bolts, screwdrivers or comets in a row you win. The nutmegs were worth a dollar, the screw drivers were worth twenty dollars, the comets were worth a thousand and the lightning bolts were worth fifty thousand dollars.
He took the Quarter, which was worn and smooth to the touch. It was darker than his other Quarters and he hoped that it's mojo would bring him luck. He scratched the first box.

 Lightning bolt.

 His breath quickened. He rolled the delicious fantasy over in his head. Fifty thousand dollars would get him a decent car and pay off his student loans. Maybe even his credit card bills too. Plus, he could put some money down on a house and ask Anita to marry him. He could buy some decent running shoes and get new glasses. His mind reeled with pleasure and possibility.

He scratched the second box.

Lightning bolt.

His heart quickened just a little and his denial kicked in. No way could this be a winner. He just didn't have that kind of luck. All the while he was thinking beneath that cynical acceptance, thinking and wishing and hoping that it was true with the simple faith of a child. But the adult in him didn't want to mess up the karma, so he continued to tell himself that there was no way a person like him would ever win 50 k. Not that he was superstitious.

Even though he knew he would be crushed when he scratched the third box, he was grateful for the hope that the five dollars had brought him. He thought about what he would do with fifty thousand dollars and decided it wouldn't really be enough to get him to where he really needed to be.

But it would get him closer.

He took his Quarter and began to scratch the third box.

March 1991
Devon, MINNESOTA

Kevin Steach awoke gradually from a dream that wasn't really a dream but a half dream that danced to the real sounds of the morning. The headache he felt was from too much pot and too much candy late at night and the dream had been vivid and intense. Unfortunately, it dissipated like smoke as he opened his eyes. He was on the verge of remembering, when he came fully away, staring at the bong on his bedside table and the field of candy wrappers looking like miniature silver boulders on some foreign planet.

 He could sense the snow outside, he could sense the cold, even though his little house was heated by only a small front room furnace. He wondered of his headache was from carbon monoxide. That furnace was pretty old. It had the smooth lines of the late 1940s. His bedroom was a mess, clothes strewn about. His feet were cold and the bottoms of his sleeping pants felt damp. He wondered anxiously if he had wet the bed, but they didn't feel wet, just damp and clammy.

The room was bright and his bed was warm, but the need to piss was great and so Kevin jumped out of bed, as was his habit, and went into the bathroom. While pissing, he could look out the window to gauge last night's heavy snow. The ground was covered and still pristine. There were no cars out yet, and the morning was blue and yellow inside his small bathroom.

The coffee maker was perking, gurgling, filling the little house with a delicious morning smell. Kevin almost did not notice the odd thing at first. It started with his feet suddenly finding icy cold wet spots on the carpet. He looked up at the ceiling but could see not leaks. A draft of cold air followed, and he turned to see his front door was slightly ajar.

"What is this," Kevin said half aloud, but instantly he rationalized that he must not have shut it tight enough when he went to bed last night. He had done that before. One morning last summer when he woke up the door was wide open. It gave him a strange feeling, as if he had been violated, but of course it had been his own fault.

And that was surely the case now, except when he went to close the door he looked outside and saw something peculiar. There in the snow on the porch at the foot of his door was a melted circle; a perfectly formed hole in the snow that stood out against the perfection of the untouched surroundings. Something shiny was at the bottom of the hole in the snow. As he reached down to see what it was Kevin saw something else. At first, he thought that the snow had been melting from his roof and dripping down around the perimeter. But looking again Kevin realized that it wasn't dripping but footprints in the snow ringing the outside of his house.

He stepped outside into the sharp air and his heart squirmed in his chest. He could clearly see footprints, what looked like all kind of different footprints in the snow around his house. It was as if someone had walked around and around his house all night long. Then he realized that someone HAD walked around and around his house all night long, the footprints were proof of that, and this filled him with a sudden jolt of terror. He could see that they were not just one set of footprints either, there was different sizes and shapes. Kevin's chest filled with a sudden dread. He quickly backed into the house.

The living room furnace was kicking on as Kevin slammed the front door shut. It cracked and popped reassuringly filling the room with an aggressive heat. Kevin was breathing heavily. He walked restlessly from room to room trying to figure out what was going on. He was chagrinned to feel so jangled by this. Everything was all right. Nothing had been disturbed. Possibly it had been a meter reader or

Something slumped against the house outside with a thump. Again, Kevin's heart slammed in his chest. He looked upward and listened to the wind picking up. He pulled on his boots, which were wet and cold and put on his coat and stepped outside. The footprints were still there but the sudden wind had begun to obscure them in places. He could plainly see that there were several different feet involved. As if a group of people had silently circled his house. He followed the footprints all around. It was only then that he noticed there were no footprints leading to or away from his house. It was as if they just appeared on his porch and circled.

The porch.

He remembered the strange hole in the snow and the glint of something beneath. When he returned there, his own footprints had trampled the spot but digging down he saw the glint again. It was a Quarter. He looked at it closely. 1963D. *That was the year I was born*, he thought to himself, then he looked all around him, all there was, was wind. He looked to see if anyone was watching him, waiting to jump out at him and laugh.

June 1992
New York, NEW YORK

Lisa Higbee walked as if in a trance down seventh avenue, looking for a pay phone. The cacophony and swirl of midtown Manhattan was oblivious to her as she concentrated on the sidewalk. She wondered how many famous people had walked this sidewalk. She wondered if it was the same sidewalk that the wits of the Algonquin Round table had walked on, or had they replaced it like they replaced the street lamps?

The cracks in the sidewalk were canyons filled with the detritus of several hundred years of the center of history. She wished she could shrink herself into them, to see the tiny civilizations that thrived under our blind and ignorant noses. Lisa didn't know why she was thinking these things. She needed to find a pay phone.

The first bank of pay phones she came to were filled with people all talking at once, oblivious to one another, the swirl and cacophony of their lives bouncing off one another rather than intersecting. That was okay though. That was fine. Lisa didn't know how she felt or how she should feel. She just needed to find a phone. She needed to call her mother. Right now.

As she came to Times Square, she waited to cross at forty seventh street. She looked at the statue of George M. Cohan in the middle of Broadway. He was covered with a caul of bird shit but he still kept smiling. Directly across from his smile was a bank of pay phones.

Lisa crossed the street carefully. She had seen too many cabs hit tourists on this corner to even think about crossing against the light. It was a warm April day. Times Square smelled like the State fair back home in South Dakota. It smelled like popcorn and hot dogs, gasoline and shit, sweet candy and perfume all rolled into one thing. A man was shaking a bundle of incense at her. Five dollars. The smell of it made her sick.

The bank of pay phones was entirely empty. For a moment, Lisa was afraid that they were broken. It was rare to see a whole bank of pay phones empty. She picked one up and heard the dial tone. She dug out a dime from her purse, then remembered that pay phones cost a Quarter now. She put the dime back and fished for a Quarter, finding an older one at the bottom of her purse. She looked at the date, like she did sometimes with coins that felt old.

She dialed her mother back at her tiny apartment on Pearl street. It rang four times until her mother picked up the phone.

"Mom?"

"IIi honcy. How did it go?"

As if choreographed, people started filling the empty pay phone booths in order, starting with right next to her. Lisa thought it looked like something from a Broadway musical.

 It was enchanting.

"Lisa? How did it go?" Her mother's voice now carried a note of urgency.

Lisa started to cry. She was happy, but she wanted to cry.

"It's a boy. The ultrasound showed it's a boy," she sobbed, letting the spring sun warm the tears on her upturned face.

July 2, 1993
Gettysburg, PENNSYLVANIA

The black smoke from the battlefield hung heavy in the thick July air. It drifted, suspended like a miasma draping the clipped carpet-like green lawns and neatly trimmed symmetrical hedges. The wave of gray had just halfheartedly charged their blue wool clad foes, hollering and shouting, rifles cracking. Moans filled the air, punctuated by the pops of small arms fire. Horses snorted and men screamed in pain. Overhead a helicopter flew in, dissipating the thick black smoke and removing them all from the moment.

It had been a hundred and thirty summers ago when this battle had been fought for real. A hundred and sixty thousand men faced off over three days and when it was over, it rained for a week. Some say the black battle smoke seeded the clouds. That might be useful someday. And just like that the world had changed.

Private Chet Bean from the Richmond Grays, stood in line to buy a Mt. Dew. Strictly speaking Mt. Dew wasn't exactly around during the Civil War, but Chet was thirsty and he didn't set the point in taking things too far. Some guys were hardcore, insisting on complete and utter accuracy. They would explode in historical indignation if their reality was compromised by so much as a plastic lighter or a filtered cigarette or a reference to Pamela Anderson.

 But Chet was thirsty after having run at top speed after a man named Trey who was portraying General George Pickett. Trey, a golf ball diver from Maryland ("white gold dude') took his role as Pickett seriously. He carefully curled his scraggly mullet into the precious curls Pickett wore in a daguerreotype Trey carried around with him. In the photo, Pickett looks like a cross between Krusty the Clown and a Klingon, which fitted Trey perfectly.

Trey led the charge enthusiastically, his brilliant and brand spanking new grey uniform with yellow piping, made from organic wool, was soaking up his sweat like a sponge. He was unsteady on his horse. a bay mare named Alanis, who did not like the commotion she was forced to dwell amidst. Later Trey became so heavy from his sweat soaked wool uniform that he passed out quite dramatically while waving a sword around his head near the stone wall and was taken to the corn dog stand and revived by a pair of women in ringlets and bustles brandishing a bottle of bright blue Gatorade.

Chet found himself in line at the turkey leg booth where a man dressed as a union cook was bellowing quaint phrases from bygone times while handing out five-dollar turkey legs. All Chet wanted was a cold Mt. Dew.

"Well, well," sneered the Union Man. "Looky what we got here. A Johnny Reb lost his unit. You surrendering Reb?"

Chet smiled. he liked to try and stay in character. "Can I just get a Mt. Dew please?" He held out a dollar bill. The union man, thrust a turkey leg into Chet's face.

"No thanks," Chet said dryly. Just the Mt. Dew. It's hot. Were you in the charge? I mean I was running up the hill toward you guys...it sure is hot out there..."

The Union Man scratched his head and readjusted his blue kepi cap. "I don't know what this Mt. Dew is you're talking about Reb, but I can give you a shot of Mr. Pembroke's new elixir and tonic called Cocoa Coala. It refreshes."

"Okay," Chet said, playing along. "How much?"

"That'll be just one quarter. Just twenty-five cents."

Chet dug in his butternut trousers that he found at Goodwill for three dollars. He withdrew a Quarter and offered it to the union man. The Union Man set down the Dixie cup of warm Pepsi on the counter and frowned at the coin.

"This Quarter isn't period. It's from 1963, not 1863." He said to Chet in a flat, almost disappointed voice.

"Are you serious?" Chet as incredulously. "I just saw you sell a turkey leg to a guy with a modern five-dollar bill!"

"Yes, but he was loyal to the Union." The Union Man said.

 Chet couldn't believe it. A wet boom behind him signaled the artillery barrage and Barbeque with karaoke. The Union Man smiled and poured the Dixie cup full of warm Pepsi onto the ground. He gave Chet back his future Quarter and offered a turkey leg to a man in a white Orkin Pest Control jumpsuit, who was carrying a basket full of bloody rubber arms and feet.

September 1994
<u>Columbus OHIO</u>

The local Green Thumb Group was a woefully misguided program to help out old drunks who had, at one time, been in the armed services. Through the years at Central High School the Night Crew had to endure quite a few of these old guys, including Oliver, who once cooked the crew an entire pot roast dinner which the crew refused to eat because he cleaned bathrooms without rubber gloves. There was old George, who every day at three o'clock would come into the keepout and retch over the trash can, using his fingers and hands to dislodge promethean gobs of rubber cement-like mucous and drop them with a thud into the trash can.

Then there was Ralph.

He was a crusty old sailor from WW2 and he didn't like anything or anyone. Darrell made him wander around outside picking up trash. That way Darrell had more time to smoke. Ralph set forth every day with an old green five-gallon plastic pickle bucket and a pair of Nifty Nabbers ™, which acted like an extended mechanical arm.

Ralph would make his way all around the school and its grounds, taking his time, picking up trash, stopping for a cigarette, taking in the day. He worked a lazy ellipse and took his time, venturing down through the heavily littered side streets through clots of stoners and ditchers who taunted him and abused him. One pimply kid demanded a cigarette from Ralph and when he refused, the kid said, "You suck!"

Ralph was flabbergasted.

"Why would anyone say something like that to me?" He'd ask, hurt and mystified. "I don't suck."

One day Ralph was standing right outside the frickin school when a fistful of change came flying out the window and hit him on the head. He bent over to pick up the coins which were mostly pennies, along with a single Quarter. He spurned the pennies in his pain, but pocketed the Quarter. He had a bruise there for a week and goddamn if it didn't hurt like a sumbitch.

Ralph went storming up there, green plastic pickle bucket and all, stamping up three flights of stairs to confront the goddamn teacher who allowed such mischief to reign in her goddamn classroom. After raving at Mrs. Hurtado's twelfth grade Health class Ralph figured he had showed them how the cow ate the cabbage and left to go find Darrell and have a smoke, but Darrell, who avoids any kind of conflict, smoked alone, hiding out on the football field.

Ralph decided he would keep that Quarter. he would keep it and find out who threw it at him and then he would make whoever did it, eat the Quarter. He didn't care if it got him fired or even arrested.

One day Ralph found a cruddy used condom in his journeying, right there in the parking lot. He was thunderstruck. His eyes blinked behind his magnifying eyeglasses. He was instantly a man transformed. He reached into his pants pocket and ran his finger along the Quarter. It was smooth and its touch comforted him in his excitement. After this thunderous revelation Ralph would lean on his Nifty Nabbers ™ and watch the teenage girls bounce by.

"Jesus Christ," he'd mutter raggedy. "Jesus Christ they're all aprobably fuckin' like crazy." He started sighing loudly at inappropriate moments. He took to flipping the Quarter in his hand, like George Raft used to do in the movies. He was going to make it be his Thing. The girls smiled at him as they bounced by, watching him expertly flipping the coin in the air and catching it single handed.

That limp, dripping rubber had galvanized Ralph and aroused what was left of his libido and soon he was confiding to John that he often fell asleep with his hand on his girlfriend's "puzzy". The girlfriend in question was a deaf, matronly 72-year-old woman who lived in the same assisted living home that Ralph did.

It was the fortuitous discover of a box of condoms in the health room (the very room of Ralph's previous meltdown, oh irony of ironies) on the third floor that gave the Night Crew the ideas for planting rubbers for Ralph.

 At first, they just tore open the foil packs and left the rubber laying in the parking lot for Ralph to find on his daily patrol, but soon they were striving for realism by experimenting with various sperm substitutes, such as Bubble Buster ™ and Creme Kleen ™, which were the only slimy white fluids they had in their cleaning supplies. Finally, after careful mixing and experimenting for texture they perfected their cum-filled rubbers and took great pains to strategically place them for Ralph to find, to best advantage.

The first one Ralph found had about a half- pint of viscous white fluid in it and Ralph was so excited he ran to the lunchroom while John and Darrell were cleaning it and triumphantly held up the bulging rubber for them on the end of his Nifty Nabber ™ for the entire gawking lunchroom to admire.

Like all the jests and japes of the Night Crew, they soon grew tired of this game and so decided to let Ralph in on it, to crush his feeble longings and disperse any remaining dreams he might have cherished.

One day Darrell came to work to find John and Ralph sitting in the keepout. Ralph was practicing his coin move.

"What are you doing that cheap trick for?" John asked him. John was always demanding to know people's motives. He liked the way it put them on the defensive.

"I got my reasons," Ralph said mysteriously.

Darrell sat down.

"You'll never guess what I found today," Ralph crowed as he punched in.

"A condom." Darrell said wearily.

"Nope," Ralph shook his head. Darrell and John could tell he wasn't even listening. He licked his lips compulsively. He wiped his palms on his polyester pants. "A goddamn used johnnybag all fulla spunk!"

"I bet it was a black one," Darrell said. The rubber had indeed been black.

"Nope. It was black." Ralph said. His eyes were wild and glittering behind the smoked lenses of his glasses.

John looked at Darrell and started laughing his wet smokers laugh.

"I put it there Ralph." Darrell said in a frank, no nonsense manner so it would have the extra weight of Truth.

"The hell you did!" Ralph blanched.

Darrell went outside and pulled the rubber out of the Dumpster and brought it down to the keepout swinging it around. Ralph backed away as if he were swinging a cobra at him. John was laughing as Darrell squeezed the rubber and rubbed Bubble Buster between his fingers. Ralph started coughing. His face turned purple.

"You some kinda queer?" He snarled as he staggered up the stairs. He edged away from Darrell to go outside and have a cigarette with the ditchers and stoners to calm his nerves.

Ralph had now thrown down a gauntlet and the Night Crew rose to the occasion. From that point on they were merciless. One of Patrick and Chris's masterpieces was two bras, stolen from the girl's locker room, liberally sprinkled with bubble buster, and nine cum filled rubbers, strewn about. For an added touch, Dan added some red food coloring blood drops.

"Jesus Fucking Christ," Ralph wheezed the next day, agog.

Ralph started wearing particularly smelly aftershave and he was also tucking in his 1940s sports shirts into his high-waisted polyester dress pants. He spent less time picking up trash and more time combing his newly dyed hair, like the Fonz.

The girls kept smiling at him as he flipped his Quarter, grinning at their big bouncy chests and tight jiggly butts, but Ralph did not know they were laughing at him and not with him.

The Night Crew lost interest in Ralph and the Rubbers when, in a creative frenzy started by the combustive combination of beer drinking, marijuana smoking and the fortuitous cooking of hotdogs, that Patrick and Chris created the ultimate Ralph rubber. They took and bite off a hot dog, smeared it with ketchup and jammed it into the rubber. The result was extremely hard to look at for more than a few seconds at a time. They proudly left it on Herb's desk so he, as their building manager, could best decide its proper placement. Instead, Herb just threw it away because he didn't want to get into any trouble.

Ralph never saw it.

As the Night Crew went on to other pursuits and interests, Ralph found no more rubbers, and like a beautiful flower deprived of sunshine and water, his color faded with his hair dye, he wilted and started to dry up. The shirts came untucked and he stopped shaving. He started limping around the parking lot again with his Nifty Nabbers ™ and his green plastic pickle bucket, darkly muttering about the goddamn kids. He flipped his Quarter no more and no one knew what became of it, although Chris said he saw Ralph use it to buy a pop in the gym lobby.

June 1995
<u>Grant Township, IOWA</u>

Jason had driven out early in the morning, unsure of exactly where he was going. He had directions from the internet but they were vague. The Iowa countryside was heavy with green, and the air was full of summer cicadas and cottonwood puffballs. The two-lane highway he was driving on was like a blue ribbon cutting through a giant lawn. All around him were corn fields and silos. He could see side roads only as he was passing them

He knew to drive north from the Mason City airport five miles away. He had spent last evening at the Surf Ballroom, soaking in the ambience, trying to put himself there on that frigid night thirty-six years ago; the very night he was born. And because Jason was born on that night, he felt a special connection these places, almost a bond. He always wondered about reincarnation.

The summer morning was so vivid and bright and the heat had not yet set in. Jason drove with his windows down deeply inhaling the farm fresh air, trying to imagine what it looked like all stubbly and frozen, like the night he was born.

Jason had done his research, and he had determined that while he had been born in California and this had happened here, in Iowa, because of the time difference the two events happened almost simultaneously. He tried in vain to get his mother to confirm this,

but she was vague ion the exact time of his birth. ("It was late at night, okay? I was on painkillers for Christ's sake!")
Jason had studied the pictures intently. The ball of wreckage, the three bodies with drifted snow around them. As he looked around him, he couldn't believe that something like that could happen in such a beautiful and peaceful place. The sun was shining and the morning birds were singing. Jason felt like he was in a margarine commercial.

Suddenly there it was, a huge pair of black glasses on the side of the road. Jason pulled over. He got out and locked his truck up. He knew we would have a good hike ahead of him. He crossed the highway over to the glasses. They were metal and were welded to a frame embedded in concrete. Jason could see a lane through the cornfield.

A trail.

 He started walking.

Heavy rains and central pivot irrigation has ensured that the corn had grown amazingly tall for late June. Jason felt like he was walking down a corridor. It was still cool amid the corn, the night chill still lingered, dissipating in the sunbeams like incense smoke. Jason kept his eyes on the ground, hard packed black dirt that evidently had seen many footfalls.

Despite the coolness Jason started to sweat as he made his way along the rows of corn and the old ragged wire fence line. He realized that this fence had played a major role in what happened. It had stopped the plane, throwing three of the four people on the plane onto the hard ground at two hundred miles an hour.

Up ahead, Jason saw a clearing and a splash of bright color. Flowers. A space had been cleared of corn and there was a steel monument, three shiny records mounted on a cement base. It had their names on it. Jason drew in a breath. He tried hard to feel something but he felt too self-conscious. He looked around him and tried to imagine what it was like to die here, right on this spot, on a cold February night in 1959. But all he felt was the joy of the beauty that was all around him. A sun splashed Iowa cornfield and the clearest bluest sky Jason had ever seen.

There were loud voices in the cornfield, raucous laughter and Jason could see a trio of drunk teenage boys staggering down the lane. Jason quickly knelt down next to the monument. He pulled out a Fender guitar pick and a Quarter and hid them among the other tributes at the base. As he stood up the boys emerged in the clearing.

"Whoa," said one, his cheeks bright red from alcohol.

"Damn dude. What a fucked-up place to die!"

Jason nodded and looked up again at the clear blue sky. The teenage boys followed his gaze, eager to see what Jason was seeing.

"What's you lookin' at up there bro?"

June 1995-March 1998

The Quarter lay at the base of the monument commemorating the untimely death of three rock and roll stars until it fell off, under the weight of many other similar tributes of quarters dimes, guitar picks, cassette tapes, flowers, pictures, and pins. There were also black plastic framed sunglasses folded neatly at the base. In time, these treasures were either stolen or scattered, and within a year the Quarter had migrated from the base of the monument to about a hundred feet into the cornfield. It wasn't buried in the ground, but it lay on the land, jostled once a year by the plowing tractor and the harvesters, but otherwise at rest. It lay in the exact same spot where Ritchie Valens body lay that cold night so many years ago.

The Quarter spent four winters on the spot where the boy had died, occupying a fraction of the earth that still held the molecules of his blood. In the summer the corn grew up high and the Quarter was shrouded in green darkness, sleeping, until one crisp March day it was found and picked up by Martin Lewis, a worker from Gamma, Georgia, who also pocketed an odd piece of metal that looked like it might have come from an airplane or something.

July 1998
Eugene, OREGON

Mike and his little son Evan walked down the hot sidewalk toward the strip of little shops right off the old campus. The shops were the typical college town places, little cafes, skateboard and cd shops, a clothing boutique. Mike and Evan lived in an old Victorian house just around the corner from this quaint hub of campus life.

Evan was three and Mike loved to watch him as they walked, his little eyes sparkling with interest, taking in all his surroundings, living in that moment entirely, instead of projecting ahead of looking back. He did not know he could love and care for another being as much as he loved and cared for this little boy, who toddled ahead of him, fearless and engaged.

Mike murmured a warning to Evan, who was growing bolder and weaving along the sidewalk. Mike was worried Evan would dash into the street, as he was working up a head of steam. The day was hot, typical August, and the heat rising up from the sidewalk had its own summer smell, a smell Mike knew would be in Evan's mind for years to come. Maybe he would remember this day, this moment every time he smelled the hot sidewalk and the street and the cut grass and blooming weeds. Mike knew these things triggered his own summer memoires from decades ago. He marveled at the majestic simplicity of the Cycle.

Evan suddenly stopped and bent over unsteadily, picking at something on the pavement. Caught daydreaming, Mike stopped short and said, in his most warning tone.

"Eeevvaaannnn."

Evan said nothing, but continued, bent in half, to pick something up from the sidewalk. He held it aloft, triumphantly, a Quarter.

"Treasure!" Evan proclaimed, his face and eyes full of joy and pride.

"Treasure." Mike agreed.

November 26, 2000
Security, COLORADO

81-year-Old Man Murders Son on Thanksgiving (AP)

A Thanksgiving Day squabble about an oil change on the family car ended in tragedy when 81-year-old Erius Oscar bludgeoned and killed his 41-year-old son Kevin. Kevin, a comic book artist from Colorado Springs, was visiting his parents for the holiday with his twin brother Karl. Witnesses say that the elder Oscar and his son had been arguing all day over petty matters. After eating they got into a heated exchange about who would change the oil in the father's car. According to witness accounts, Kevin told his father he was "through taking (expletive deleted) from his father and was going to stand up to him like a man." The elder Oscar, who told police that he paid both of his son's rent and car payments, allegedly threw a Quarter at his son Kevin as "payment" for changing the oil. The son caught the Quarter and put it in his pocket. When the elder Oscar demanded it back suddenly and his son refused, the father went to his tool bench, took out a claw hammer and struck his son repeatedly in the head. He then sat down calmly in a lawn chair and awaiting authorities, who found him rocking in the chair, saying he had hurt his son. He was then taken into custody. The claw hammer and the Quarter were taken into custody as evidence. Erius Oscar will be

arraigned December 2nd by El Paso District Attorney
J. Dewayne Farley.

February 14, 2001
<u>Truth or Consequences, NEW MEXICO</u>

Terry passed the Ninth Avenue Arcade every morning when she drove to her school bus driving job. It was a job she hated, but she had no choice. She had been working as a school bus driver for almost twenty years and if she wanted to retire, she had to stick it out another few years. Her hatred of bus driving was also due to the fact that she was forced to get this job when her husband Hermie divorced her without warning and went to live in Portland, Oregon with a woman he met on the internet.

After he left, she had gone through all of his emails, discovering, much to her horror, that he had been quite active in xxx chat rooms with other women, girls even, and had saved the chats, for whatever reason. Hermie had been a good husband, inoffensive and obedient, but he had controlled everything in their lives and upon his absence, Terry had to deal with the raw and bleak financial outlook that he had hidden from her for so long.

The graphic nature of his saved chats disturbed her on a profound level. She and Hermie had a very regimented sex life; every Tuesday afternoon she would accommodate him and his needs. Wasn't that enough for him? After her initial shame and anger had cooled, she had to admit to herself, if not to the universe, that no, it had not been enough for him.

And now, almost seven years later, as she drove by the Ninth Avenue Arcade, a nondescript brick building with no windows right next to Lasso Liquors, she found herself wondering if it had been enough for her too. She chastised herself; a middle aged, post-menopausal woman, thinking about dirty sex and wondering what it was like in that pink and yellow concrete cube.

She had never even seen any pornography until she had clicked on a few of Hermie's favorite links and discovered that he liked seeing pictures of women with two men at one time, pictures of women with semen all over their faces, pictures of women with women. Terry had flushed and fumed at these images, her blood ran hot but her anger and shame at what the images implied was almost too much for her to bear.

She found herself thinking about those images while she was driving her bus full of screaming kids every day. As they carried on, raising a din not unlike that of a crippled jet engine, Terry's mind was imagining wet vaginas stuffed with spurting penises. She wondered if she was going crazy. She remembered that her mother had always told her that old women sometimes turned nasty. Terry wondered if it was finally happening to her.

At night her mind was a swirl and she found herself going back to the computer and staring at the images hungrily. She began masturbating a lot, several times a day, much to her shame. She started off using just her hand, but soon graduated to her electric shaver, buffeted by a washcloth. When that failed to get the job done, she moved on to an old hand sander her husband used to use. She had to be careful with that however.

It was on Valentine's day that she made up her mind. Her mind. It's like it wasn't hers anymore, but like it had been taken over by her desires, which coursed through her like a pulse, no that's not right, like a tide, ebbing and flowing, sometimes flooding her sometimes rolling back to expose the hard sandy bottom with all its rocks and wreckage.

She drove by the Ninth avenue Arcade on her way to work and was filled with a delicious feeling of naughtiness, knowing that she had made up her mind to just try it, to just see. What could that hurt? She was a grown woman, she was curious. She had no man in her life, no reason not to except some stupid invisible line that she felt she should never cross. Why the heck not? What difference did it make anyway? It's not like her life was anything to holler about now.

By the time she got her bus back into the yard she was giddy and excited. people even commented to her on her buoyant behavior.

"Got a beau?" One of the other bus drivers asked her, a nasty tone hidden in the mix if her voice. Terry laughed it off, but it had struck something deep inside of her and in that spot she had started to slowly, infinitesimally, bleed.

The last afternoon was slipping into evening and as she drove past the restaurant with their overflowing valentines' day customers, she felt the pang of being alone. She wondered if she was becoming depraved. She decided to pretend to herself that she was going to just spontaneously decide to stop in. Not like she had planned it or anything. Not at all. Just a lark Tra la la.

The small parking lot was dirt and gravel. there were about five other cars. A bright street light shone down at the entrance. Terry though it was odd that the building had no windows and only one door. Taking a breath, she ever so nonchalantly opened the heavy metal door which screeched and squealed. A blast of bleachy heat hit her face as she entered a brightly lit store. This wasn't so bad, she though, smiling, staring straight ahead. She noted the presence of a bored looking woman, about her own age, flipping through a magazine and smoking a cigarette. Terry noted other people milling around looking intently at the items on the shelves.

And WHAT items! Dildos, pocket pussies, blow up dolls, vibrators, it all made her head swim. It was all so out in the open, so...ordinary that she felt relief, almost a sense of suddenly being let in on a great joke of a secret.

A man was holding up a rubber dildo like he was examining a circular saw at Sears. Another man asked the bored woman behind the counter of she had any anal sex specific movies. Terry saw the third man leafing through a DICKS AND CHICKS MAGAZINE when she inhaled sharply, recognizing him as a third-grade teacher at Buddy Holly Elementary. He felt her eyes and looked up, but she could see no recognition in his face. He looked right at her, but Terry felt oddly safe.

She began to become aware that people were coming from the back part of the room, through a pair of black curtains. She guessed that the store continued all the way back and that maybe the items behind the curtain were even more salacious and offensive. But when she went through the curtains, all she saw was a series of cubicles, each with their own black curtain.

Terry's eyes dilated in the darkened corridor as she immediately realized that things could happen in these cubicles. She heard sounds, shufflings, mechanical sounds she didn't even want to image. She took a few steps, noting the bleachy odor and humid air. Before her was an open cubicle, its curtain drawn to the side.

Terry entered and quickly drew the curtain. Inside was a chair and an old fashion moviola machine that looked like a cross between a videogame and an antique. Her heart was pounding and she felt herself smiling. Her body throbbed. The room was very dark and she sensed people all around her yet she felt totally, deliciously, alone.

She pulled out a coin and inserted it into the slot of the machine. The tiny screen flickered to life, showing a huge breasted woman, in 60s style and with the color washed out, sucking off a large panting dog. The woman kept sucking, looking toward the camera and winking until the dog started thrusting its hips. Then the screen went dark.

Terry sat in the dark, shivering and breathing, every breath and orgasm every shiver an ejaculation, her total being was throbbing. It was the most wonderful, horrible thing she had ever gotten herself into and she gave herself to it completely. She was groping her breasts, rubbing her crotch like a wild, crazy woman. She wished she had that hand sander.

She stood up, brushing something against the wall. She fished out her last Quarter and popped it into the coin slot. The screen lit up the booth like a tiny strobe and Terry watched as the dog now mounted the woman and Terry was treated to a close up of the dog's knot firmly in place in the woman's pussy. She forced herself to look away and in the moment before the screen went dark again, she noticed the holes in the wall and while wondering what their purpose was, she suddenly found out, right as the flickering light went out.

August 2001
New York, NEW YORK

The Quarter came to Ron from a regular customer; a wonky eyed speed freak named Skye, who often sold Ron coins in order to supplement his welfare income. Ron's little coin store was in an old part of downtown, in the shadow of the mighty World Trade Center. In fact, Ron's store was literally in the shadow of the two towers, meaning that his days were a twilight of eternity, the buzzing blue of fluorescents 24/7 had become part of the backdrop of Ron's life.

Even in sunny August, his store was like a permanent evening all blue and artificially lit. On this day, Skye had been waiting for Ron when he came in. Skye lived behind the service vents of Tower 1, huge grates that blew hot air in the winter and cool air in the summer. He panhandled for change and was always careful to inspect it afterward. It was simple common sense. If Skye could sell a 1947 penny to Ron for thirty-five cents, then he was making money.

In the seven years he and Ron had been doing business, Skye had found several interesting coins, including a 1919 VDB penny which Ron gave him two hundred dollars for. It was in rough shape, he said. Skye and Ron had a tumultuous relationship, with Skye often being banned, usually for casting slurs on Ron's Jewish ancestry.

Of the coins Skye brought in today, the only half interesting one was the 1963D Quarter which booked for between fifty cents and six dollars.
"Well, the only one here that's even remotely interesting is this Quarter. I'll give you a buck for it."

Skye nodded, licking his lips. He accepted Ron's dollar and left without saying anything Ron knew he would be back.

Ron inspected the Quarter with his loop and determined it was only in "good" condition. He cleaned it up a bit with a damp rag. The good thing was that it was pure silver; made before the mint used zinc and copper cores in their blank discs. Ron idly looked out his window shrouded in perpetual twilight. It was two in the afternoon.

A customer entered, a trader from up the street on his break probably. Ron reached for the key to his gold box. These guys were all buying gold lately. The Trader nodded and picked up the Quarter that was laying on the counter. Ron had by now placed it in a small white cardboard frame, encasing the coin in cellophane. On it he had written: "1963D Good Condition. $2.00"

The Trader looked at it and smiled at Ron. "Ever wonder what these coins would say if they could talk?" He asked, but his question was drowned out by a low flying plane. Ron shrugged and pulled out the Gold.

January 2002
New York, NEW YORK

new york craigslist > for sale / wanted > collectibles
please flag with care: [?]

miscategorized
prohibited
spam/overpost
best of craigslist
Avoid scams and fraud by dealing locally! Beware any deal involving Western Union, Moneygram, wire transfer, cashier check, money order, shipping, escrow, or any promise of transaction protection/certification/guarantee. *More info*
cntirc coin storc inventory

Date: 2002-01-30,   8:23PM   EST
Reply to: see below [Errors when replying to ads?]

entire inventory of small NYC coin store destroyed in 9/11 attacks. Thousands of coins, ingots, stamps ,medals and other small collectibles. has to be seen to be believed. serious inquiries only.
Location: NYC
it's NOT ok to contact this poster with services or other commercial interests

PostingID: 201770122
Top of Form
Bottom of Form

November 2003
<u>Swindon, Wiltshire, UK</u>

The 1963D Quarter now lay, inert, wrapped and stapled into a cardboard frame, in a glass case, surrounded by other captured and imprisoned coins, suffocating in their own polythene wrappings. Bought in New York by an English tourist named Lonnie Pretsmore as a last-minute souvenir of a once in a lifetime vacation, the Quarter soon made its way through a maze of dilettante coin collectors until it ended up in a little coin shop in Swindon.

The display case it was in was very old, almost two hundred years. It was oak and glass, with many modifications; such as florescent light bars that seared the coins surfaces and exposed all of their faults along with all of their beauty.

Next to the 1963D Quarter was a 1914 Half Crown, that had once been owned by Charlie Chaplin's father. There was an Australian coin that had come from the belly of a Great White Shark. Also occupying the shelf was an 1878 shilling that had once passed through Jack the Ripper's slimy hands. A Roman coin from the year Christ died; a mute witness to the execution of St. Peter. There was a silver ingot, minted in the reign of Henry the seventh and fondled by his granddaughter Elizabeth. There was a Kennedy Half Dollar that had spent its entire existence in a sock drawer of Christian Banas Jr. in Lynwood, New Hampshire.

Of course, these were only the interesting coins. There were many others, old and new, each with a long and complicated trail. An American Silver dollar that had been buried with a murdered settler and later dug up by Indians and traded for whiskey. A French coin that had been found in a beautiful field by a man with a new metal detector, who did not realize that the fine field he prospected had once been a horror filled trench from the Great War. That would also explain all the bullets and empty cans he also found there.

There were ancient Chinese coins, with their indecipherable markings and odd shapes, some so old their purposes were obscured. There were pirate coins, doubloons and pieces of eight, popular sellers, all. There was another American Silver dollar from 1882 that was known as an "opium dollar" because it's face swung open on a micro hinge revealing a hollowed-out space used to supposedly smuggle opium.

The tiny doorbell tinkled as a customer entered the tiny shop. The owner, Ronald Wessley, emerged from a back room. The coin store had been in his family for two generations. His father, Ronald Sr. had died only seven years ago and his son was sure his ghost haunted the basement, where sacks of coins lay on damp corners, waiting to be put out into the light. He stood behind the counter and nodded at the man who had entered. The man looked around self-consciously and then focused his attention on the glass case.

"Can I have a look at that one?" He pointed and Ronald reached in and withdrew a 1963D Quarter.

The customer turned the coin around in his hand. It wasn't anything special. He didn't understand American money all that well. He handed the coin back, shrugging, and pointed to a doubloon.

"How about that? A piece of pirate booty eh?"

Ronald replaced the Quarter and pulled out the doubloon and handed it over. Always with the doubloons. Ronald had scores of them. They were his best sellers.

"Amazing," The customer marveled, turning the coin around in the light with his fingers.

May 2004
Bremen, GERMANY

Dot was walking down the boulevard on this beautiful spring day. She was looking forward to beginning work in her garden. She loved to work in the ground, to watch things grow. It connected her to the Earth in a way that nothing else did. And even though she now walked down a paved street full of concrete buildings, she still could smell the fragrant earth awakening from a deep and cold winter's sleep.

As Dot stopped to cross a busy street, she played a game with herself. She searched for one spot of bare ground; something with dirt. As she waited for the traffic top allow her to cross, she looked everywhere around her, but it was all concrete, cobblestone or brick.

She started to cross the street, feeling vaguely disappointed and not wanting to feel the brightness of this spring day dim even a little bit. She could smell wet dirt, the smell of spring, she was sure, but she got to the other side of the street, it was as solid and manmade as the other.

Then she noticed the planter next to the crossing walk. It was filled with freshly turned dirt, no doubt in preparation for its yearly seeding of flowers. Dot's heart leaped and she peered into the planter, inhaling the fragrance of the wet black dirt within.

Dot saw a coin on the planter, looking for all the world like someone had left it there just for her. She picked it up. It was an

American coin, from 1963, but that's all she knew about it. She felt it was a lucky thing, and put it in her pocket, as she made her way west, toward open land.

Later, at home, when she went to put her blue jeans into the wash, she looked for the coin in her pockets, but it wasn't there.

She wondered about it for the rest of the night.

May 2004-January 2006

The Quarter made its way across Europe, mostly as a curio. In the summer of 2004, it was off the warm coast of Spain, where it was dropped by a nervous French tourist while snorkeling off shore. Frightened by a school of leech fish, the tourist dropped his waterproof fanny pack onto the ocean floor, scattering its contents like a tiny shipwreck. In time the Quarter washed up on shore and was found by a small boy named Javier, who hid it under his pillow.

The Quarter was eventually traded by Javier to his friend Sam, who in turn lost the Quarter in a washing machine that wasn't calibrated for American coins. It remained in the machine until the fall of 2005 when it was freed by a Basque repairman and pocketed surreptitiously by the aforementioned repairman, who had never before seen American money and wondered who the woman was depicted on the coin.

The Quarter was given by the Basque repairman to an American tourist named Johnny Steel, a native of Forks, Washington, who was vacationing in Spain with his girlfriend Julie. The Basque repairman observed the tourists in a cafe and was suddenly moved to present them with their native coin as a gesture of good will. Unfortunately, the couple did not know the meaning of this gesture and were half insulted. They thanked the Basque repairman for this gesture anyway and spent the day wondering what the meaning was behind it, coming to several sinister conclusions and they spoke about it late into the night, where they pondered the journey of a coin that had been around for so long

August 2006
Eugene OREGON

The donut shop was brightly lit.

Mal Lipik sipped his sweet brown coffee and wiped powdered sugar across his face. Screwing up his courage, then feeling it slip down to around his ankles, he searched the red vinyl topped stools for a friend. He nervously tapped a Quarter against the counter, beating out a ragged tattoo that clearly annoyed the Waitress behind the counter.

"Why don't you go ahead and give me another one of them long johns." Mal had more coffee left than donut so he wanted to even things out. Lucy, the waitress, handed him his long john on a pink paper napkin. Mal felt sorry for her. It must be lonesome working cloudy afternoons in a donut shop. He managed an unnatural smile as Lucy poured more coffee, a smile that was so disturbing that Lucy felt a bolt of fear go through her and wondered in a flash if this man was going to murder her and hide her body in the woods for all the raccoons to claw at and eat.

"Heard some thunder." Mal said innocently, his voice flat but full of menace to Lucy, who backed off self-consciously, looking slightly ashamed. Mal stirred his coffee and felt sorry for Lucy. he felt sorry for himself. He looked at the wall between them and found it to be insurmountable. He tapped the Quarter a little more insistently. It was grating on Lucy's nerves, but she didn't dare say anything or he would surely dismember her and throw her disarticulated limbs into trash bags and throw it out for the dogs to claw at and eat.

A young girl entered, looking slightly disoriented. She looked seventeen but could have been thirty for all Mal knew. She dressed like a punk rocker, with many piercings and tattoos. Her hair was a bright and vibrant pink. In her hand she carried a well-used paper bag, the kind you get at the grocery store when you don't want to use plastic.

The girl sat down right next to Mal even though there were open stools with red vinyl tops everywhere. Mal felt his personal space was being invaded and he flushed uncomfortably. His armpits started to sweat. His Quarter tapping became more frantic and arrhythmic.

The girl ordered a chocolate donut and chocolate milk. Then she turned her full attention onto Mal and just started talking.

"I see you tapping a Quarter. It rained Quarters on my house last night. Hundreds of them. Thousands of them. It made me rich."

"She reached into the bag and pulled out a handful of quarters and dribbled them onto the counter. Mal also saw a small crowbar in the bag.

"The sky got all cloudy and pink and it just rained quarters all over my house. Is that where you got your Quarter?"

Mal shook his head no, then cleared his throat.

"You say it rained quarters? Like from the sky?"

"Yep. It sure did. See?"

Into the bag and more quarters on the counter. Lucy was getting nervous. She set down the girl's order in front of her. The girl smiled.

"Take it out of these." She said happily, chugging down the chocolate milk as if famished. Lucy dug through the Quarters until she had enough. Then looking the girl right in the eye. she scooped up another handful just for good measure.

"I don't like the medication I'm on now." She said, eating the donut. "I don't feel in control of myself. My inner self. My pumpkin brain. It's because of the big computers. But I figure that as long as you feed the machine quarters it'll leave you alone."

Mal nodded as if he understood completely, but of course he didn't. How could he? Lucy hovered behind the counter, alert. but keeping her distance, her eyes darting from Mal to the girl.

The girl finished her donut and abruptly got up. She again looked Mal square in the face.

"Do you meet many disturbed people like me?" She demanded but before he could answer, she turned violently away from him and stalked out the door and into the blooming afternoon thunderclouds. Mal and Lucy watched her go. The little donut shop was quiet and both Mal and Lucy observed that the sky was filling with ominous pink tinged thunderheads.

"I never know what to say to people like that." Mal said embarrassed and Lucy softened toward him. This was a nice man who would not rape you and leave your rotting body in the river for the snakehead fish and frogs to claw at and eat.

Lucy swept away the girl's trash and scooped up the pile of quarters left on the counter. A clap of thunder, rolling ominously, and everything went still and quiet. Mal watched her, remembering his own Quarter, which he used to resume tapping out the rhythm of his moments.

June 2007
Hardin MONTANA

Patty Negomari could barely hear herself think over the whining thrum and hum of the plane engines. Her helmet didn't help matters either. She felt as if her head was encased in cotton wadding, the sounds seemed surreal to her. This whole thing seemed surreal to her and her heart hammered with dread and excitement.

Turning forty wasn't easy for Patty. She had recently admitted to herself that her marriage to her high school sweetheart Ron was dead, and she also admitted to herself that she was too much of a coward to end it and move on. As far as she could tell Ron was oblivious, showing his boredom and anger only in the way her constantly mocked her, creating her as a cartoonish character in his own mind and treating her accordingly. She had gotten so used to it that she had actually assumed the character by and large, and hated herself for it.

Courage was her problem. Or lack of courage. So, when she turned forty that spring, she decided she would build courage, like someone building a sturdy and indestructible stone bridge. She started out with small things, like picking up spiders with a paper towel and throwing them outside. Then she graduated to stomping on spiders, killing them so that they could never ever come back to frighten her. She took walks at night around the neighborhood. She signed up for a martial arts class and in six short weeks had graduated to a green belt in kung fu.

Now she was in a small airplane over the golden plains of Montana. The surrounding mountains were stately spiky sentinels, the sky was a blue Patty had never seen reproduced, a deep comforting blue that she remembered from her childhood and from intense and vivid dreams.

The gear was very heavy and Patty sagged under the weight of it. The parachute was down past her butt, and it felt like she was hauling a dead body around with her. The goggles she wore were yellow lensed giving cheerful a golden hue to everything around her.

Suddenly, Larry, the sky diving instructor stood up, or rather crouched at the open door, something Patty had been emphatically avoiding looking at, and gestured to her to step out. Everything inside Patty screamed! no! but she shuffled forward, helped by the vibration of the plane's floor beneath her feet. She thought her chest would burst. Her heart was pounding in her throat and her mind was bordering on hysteria.

Larry smiled at her and gave her at thumbs up. The plane engine was deafening now, the vibration and the blast of wind rocked her and even with her helmet on, the wind lacerated what bare skin of her face was showing. Panicking, she moved to step back but all of a sudden, the noise and the vibration was gone and she was flying in perfect eerie silence.

Well, falling was more like it. To Patty it was as if she was floating motionless in a windy sky, except for the fact that her cheeks were flapping and her teeth were drying from the wind. The soundlessness was now replaced by a steady roar; like standing under Niagara Falls.

She looked neither up nor down, but straight ahead into the dreamy blue. She was not serene but cold, like the cold you go into when someone dies. A color caught the corner of her eye and she saw parachutes opening. She was surprised, and panicked, groping for the cord. As she did, she looked down, saw the golden ground rushing up at her. She found the cord and pulled as hard as she could, reflexively stretching her toes and bracing her feet as if to brake.

At first nothing happened and fear gripped her, but then she was jolted, so much so that she spun around like a yo yo on a string. Stupidly, she had put her cell phone and spare change on the pocket of her jumpsuit and saw it fly away from her now, the phone a black speck against the sky, the change, a nickel some pennies and a Quarter, seemed to float beside her until the filling parachute jerked her upward and slowed her descent.

She watched now, the falling items from her unzipped pocket, her eye resting on what she thought was the Quarter, as it rushed to meet the ground beneath her. She floated fast downward, and watched with excitement as the ground came up to meet her.

She hit hard and rolled over on the ground, the vivid and intense smell of weeds and dirt suddenly filling her senses. She lay on the ground panting, crying, alive. When she opened her eyes, she saw her Quarter on the ground right by her face. Then she stood up and walked away from the blue sky and into her new life.

July 2007-April 2009

The Quarter was soon enough separated from Patty Negomari and wound up in the pocket of Andy Graver in Butte. Andy spent the Quarter on two loose cigarettes from a girl in his biology class. The girl, Mary Morrison, who was supposedly the granddaughter of the Doors singer, lost the Quarter when she accidently tossed it at some squirrels in the park as she was feeding them popcorn from her jacket pocket.

A squirrel grabbed the Quarter and finding it not to be edible, buried it at the foot of a large cottonwood tree at the park. There the Quarter rested for almost a year before being flushed out by a spring thunderstorm and found by a girl named Rosa O'Brien who was looking for snakes living in the exposed roots of the giant tree.

Rosa cleaned the Quarter and kept it for a while as a curiosity until she needed to buy some eye makeup and had to scoop together all her available money. The color of the eye makeup she bought was called #9-11 Clear Sky Blue.

April 2009
Casper WYOMING

Junior Lamb was taking a nice hot foamy shower when he reached for his VO5 shampoo and slipped. Although he was agile for forty-five, he was off balance and the bottom of the tub was slippery and he went down full force, taking the shower rod and curtain slashing down with him, striking the side of the tub with his back and falling onto the tile floor beside the tub. The hot water pounded him and he struggled to catch his breath on the floor. He had the wind knocked out of him it seemed. He tried to spring up, as he had so many other times when he had slipped but his legs wouldn't work. The water pounding his back was still hot and steamy.

His whole lower body felt numb and tingly, like when his feet fell asleep underneath him at work. Junior flooded with panic. He couldn't move and the water kept pounding his back from behind, filling the room with steam. Junior was face down on the slippery bathroom floor. His hands were grasping for something. anything. The water pounding his back was hot.

Junior tried not to panic. He had never considered this scenario. His wife Laura would not be home for another eight hours. He tried again to get up and the next thing he remembered was waking up on the floor even more twisted than when he first fell. he had no memory or knew how long he had been out. The water pounding his back was getting cooler.

Shivering now, Junior tried again to crawl. He succeeded moving a few inches. Now the cold water was pounding the back of his legs. He was shivering. He shouted, but his voice got lost in the floor beneath it. he tried twisting his head and shouting for help. But his little house stood at the end of a long front yard. His closest neighbor was on the other side of an irrigation ditch. The water pounding the back of his legs was cold.

Junior tried to think, think of any way he could get help. He was sure not that he was seriously injured. The tingling had gone away, so he thought maybe he could get up.

He tried.

 Detonating megaton pain shot through his back, down his arm and into his fingers. It was a pain so sharp so clear so deep that it was almost exquisite. He collapsed again, and as the pain held him and shook him like a dog with a toy, his eyes felt calm and rested on the dirt and grime beneath his bathtub. His nostrils, snorting on the tile, blew dust bunnies and fine dirt from the floor. The water pounding on the back of his legs was icy cold.

As the pain receded slowly, like the tides of the ocean, Junior focused on underneath his bathtub. It was very dirty and mysterious. There were several dust covered slivers of soap that had popped out of his hands over the years. There were several caps from various tubes and jars. A stiffened ancient washcloth that had once been bright orange stood in a far corner like an ancient petrified pumpkin artifact. There were a few plastic razors. And something else, something silver. The water pounding on the back of his legs was very cold.

A glint caught his eye. The pain was now a low rumble, an ominous companion warning his not to try to gain control again. The pain was in control now. Junior knew that and on some level; he accepted it. He was bitter about his situation, how it had all come to this. He was scared of being paralyzed. He wept and wondered what it was he had done to deserve something like this happening to him. The water pounding on the back of his legs was so cold he couldn't feel it anymore.

Hours passed, or maybe it was just minutes. Time had taken on a different meaning for Junior. He wondered if he should just try to fall asleep until Laura got home. The silvery glint caught his eye again. Junior saw the glint as hope. In this situation one tended to see everything as a metaphor. His arm was out in front of him. It ached from the awkward position and Junior decided to try to readjust. At the same time, he would try to reach for whatever it was glinting in the grime. The water pounding on the back of his legs made a sound like rain.

Junior had to work up his courage. He had to plan. To think. Think about how he was going to do this thing. This thing he needed to do. He didn't know if the pain would allow him to move again. If it would be merciful and allow him just this readjustment or if it would bite down hard, merciless in its total control. Junior planned his moves down to the last detail. He went over and over them again in his mind. His mind was focused as it had never been. Like a laser it drilled itself in scenarios, expectations, and dry runs. The water pounding on the back of his legs was splashing on the floor all around him.

Then it happened. In one swift moment, Junior moved. He rolled and at the same time he thrust his hand farther beneath the tub and clawed frantically at the slime. He felt a coin, it felt like a Quarter, and pulled it back. This all happened in less than a second. There was a pause in the universe, then the Pain came. It burst through like an angry parent bursting through a door. It admonished Junior with its diamond hard and unforgiving severity. Junior gasped and screamed, rolling back to his previous position, dropping his Quarter. Junior heard a high-pitched whine in his head and everything started to go white. It was a pleasant sensation, and it felt like the water pounding on the back of his legs had grown warm again.

February 2010
Denver, COLORADO

When Dean packed for the hospital, he wasn't thinking about the end of his life. He wasn't looking around his bedroom thinking, this is the last time I will see that picture or this is the last time I will look at this light bulb. He was thinking about his lucky Quarter. And salt and pepper. Which he wasn't allowed to have. Sherry, his wife was in the other room, on the phone to their daughter Aggie at Fort Bragg.

"Dad has to go into the hospital again," he heard her say, her voice far away in the other room. "They want to test his heart again."

Dean sat down on the bed. He felt tired. He stuffed the salt and pepper shakers deep into the bag where Sherry wouldn't find it. He was panting on the bed. Tired. He was finding it harder and harder to care anymore. He used to be scared of dying, of dying suddenly, like he had died five years before at Rollie Ford taking the truck in for an oil change and keeling over in the lobby. For four minutes he had been in the sweet ether of the dead and he regretting not having any memory of it. When he died the first time, his fists were clenched tightly and it was only later at the hospital that they unclenched and inside of one they found his lucky Quarter.

Dean didn't remember what he had a Quarter in his fist for. What could he buy at Rollie Ford for a Quarter? That day was still hazy to him. He remembered taking the truck in. The next thing he remembered flying over the Grand Canyon and watching the rocks fight over cactus.

Man, that was some good shit they gave him in the hospital!

"Dean!" Sherry was calling from the other room. Dean grunted so she could hear him and he heard her resume her conversation with their daughter Aggie. Aggie had just gotten back from Afghanistan where, according to a letter Dean got from a major Charles W. Pierce, Aggie single handedly killed seven insurgents, saving her whole squad. To Dean she was still his little girl who didn't have enough sense to come in out of the rain. He chuckled at the image of Aggie standing, grinning in the rain, proud of not having enough sense to come in.

"...just checking oxygen levels in his blood..." He heard Sherry say and he rubbed his chest, where the pacemaker was. The times it had gone off and kicked him had scared him so badly that he began praying to God again, something he hadn't done since he was a little boy. "Okay God, I swear I'll never eat another pickle or smoke another cigarette if you only give me one more year." He wanted his grandkids to be old enough to remember him. He wondered if they thought of him as he thought of his own grandfather. The thought made him sad.

"Are you packed?" Sherry was in the doorway, her hands on her hips, looking at Dean quizzically. "Are you okay?" She asked and he could hear the alarm in her voice.

"Yeah," Dean said. "Just get me some peroxide and some duct tape." He laughed dryly but Sherry did not smile.

She didn't get it.

Dean's boy Mack was looking at him, his face was full of fear and uncertainty. He was kneeling over the sheep, who had slit her stomach open on the jagged end of the fence. The sheep bawled, it's eyes flashing with pain, its tongue lolling from its mouth, a perfect cloud of vapor mushrooming from its cries. Mack started to run toward the house, his feet crunching in the snow.

"Where are you going?" Dean asked him, examining the sheep.

The hospital room was small and high up, giving Dean a feeling of floating above the-Mile-High city. Not that he cared. It could be Calcutta for all he cared. He was sedated and watching TV. Going in and out. Jesus! Was that a man fucking a dog on TV?

Man, this is some good shit!

Dean rolled his head around. He was alone. It seemed like it was very late at night. When he looked back at the TV is was turned off. Dean laughed out loud. He wished he was this high all the time. He had been sleeping, and as the dream faded like vapor from his mind he remembered where he was, Denver, and why he was there, heart.

The doctor had told Sherry that Dean's heart was only working at 20% capacity. They agreed he was to be moved to the top of the heart transplant list. Dean had laughed out loud then too. He knew he was never going to get someone else's heart. He was 60 and he was falling apart. A new heart wasn't going to make that much difference anymore. Now if they offered him a new dick, maybe.

He didn't feel that bad. Just tired. And he didn't care anymore. About anything. But no, that's not right. He did care but he didn't

want to. He let go of wanting to care, but it drifting alongside of him like a cheerful, colorful balloon.
Man! This was some good shit!

"Where are you going?" He asked Mack, his breath mushrooming from his mouth joining with the vapor from the braying sheep below him.

"To get the gun." Mack said, breathless, his eyes darting back from the sheep to his father. There was blood on the snow. The sheep was cut deep in the belly.

"You don't need the gun," Dean said. "Bring me a bottle of peroxide and some duct tape."

Dean turned his head and looked out the small window. It was night and it was snowing. Dean liked the snow when he didn't have to deal with it. He could relax now and enjoy this great morphine high or whatever it was they had him on. He was flying.

He watched the snow, the thick flakes drifting down through the beam of an outside light. It was beautiful and Dean felt like crying but he hadn't cried since his dad died in 1985.

He wasn't sure he remembered how.

But no, that's not true, He had cried.

He had cried a lot since he died the first time. He cried at MASH episodes and insurance commercials. He cried when AC/DC songs came on the radio. He cried driving his motorcycle home past the old farm from work. He was ashamed at how soft he had become because of his injured heart. In his shame he cried again. Flooded with dread and fear which subsided quickly like a fast tide, he settled down into a formal kind of acceptance and watched the beautiful snow.

Mack ran into the house where Sherry was ironing shirts.

"Dad needs a bottle of peroxide and some duct tape. Sheep cut its belly open pretty bad..."

Mack panted, his face wild and hopeful. Sherry looked out the window and could see Dean off by the fence, kneeling over something. Shaking her head, she gathered the peroxide and the duct tape and gave them to Mack.

Mack ran back to his dad in the snow. The day was clear and crisp and the snow was like a fresh coat of frosting over their small farm. Some fool drove by on the snow-covered road on a motorcycle, filling the air with a harshness.

 Mack reached Dean and handed him the items. Acting quick, Dean poured the entire bottle of peroxide into the wound while the sheep screamed in pain. He then stood the sheep up and began wrapping duct tape around the sheep like a saddle, binding the wound closed.

"What are you doing?" Mack asked him.

"I'm fixing him." Dean said matter of factly.

"You can't fix a sheep with duct tape!"

"Wanna bet? How much you got on you?"

Mack checked his pocket. "A Quarter."

"And you know," Mack said with tears in his eyes, holding up Dean's lucky Quarter at the funeral, "That sheep went on to have twins later that spring." Everybody in the room clapped and laughed.

In the hospital room, Dean watched the snow and thought about the salt and pepper he had packed. He knew Sherry would find it. He wasn't allowed to have salt and pepper. Not even food interested him anymore. He rolled his lucky Quarter in his hand. He was comforted by its presence there.

The snow was even more furious than before.

He glanced down at the table by his bed and wondered where his salt and pepper was. When he looked up at the window, he was astonished to see it was sunny outside. Dean looked back at the TV. Holy Christ! Now there was a man with two dicks fucking twins!

Far out!

Man! This was some good shit all right!

August 2011
Bisque, NEW MEXICO

In the jar there was a nickel that had been to Vietnam. A Dime that had belonged to Richard Nixon. There were several pennies, chattering away in their cold copper language. There were other Quarters, one from 1936 that had spent almost fifty years inside wall of a restaurant. It was found by one of the men tearing the building down and used to buy a pop later that afternoon. The 1936 Quarter was almost completely smooth, its serrated edges worn down to tiny black lines barely perceptible. Its silver was also from Colorado, and the two Quarters were briefly reunited at their cores; their chemical content almost identical. They tried to reminisce, but the chatter of the pennies drowned them out until the quiet of the night came and all the coins finally quieted down.

May 2012
Tempe, ARIZONA

■ 4:21 p.m. — A report was taken about the theft of a cell phone from Commerce Way.

■ 5:00 p.m. — Police were called to Market Square for a report about a "suspicious coin." Investigating officer reported it was a quarter.

■ 5:45 p.m. — A Greenleaf Avenue caller reported someone was living under a ramp where

September 2013
Garland, CALIFORNIA

The Quarter spent two years in a library book, "Dogs of the Titanic." It was placed there by Leonard Rubin, who used the Quarter as a book mark. The Quarter was mashed between pages 342-343. On one side, the Quarter could make out the words, "paddling frantically in the icy" and on the other side it could make out the words, "skidded down the sinking stern barking."

February 2015
Greeley, COLORADO

wedged in the crack of the vinyl car seat forgotten amid crumbs, combs and debris

gasoline air cold fumes a naked butt grinding heavy breaths frosting the windows

gasoline air cold sex conception dark vinyl seat crack gasping, reaching her hand down into the seat for exquisite leverage a moment of life gasping gasoline air cold lust throbbing along with the radio night

July 2017
Omaha, NEBRASKA

"Hey I found a Quarter!"

November 2022
Verizon, OHIO

The coffee mug is old. It is white crockery with a constellation of tiny cracks in the glaze. Emblazoned in black letters across the front of the mug are the words FUCK YOU. The coffee mug no longer holds coffee, but coins, buttons, pins and other assorted accumulate thought worthy of saving. In the old coffee mug, there is a Quarter who had spent most of its time lately in virtual 4D peep shows and sensidick arcades, passing from one set of sticky fingers to another. The arcades and virtulerotica mechanics were among the last pleasure blocks to accept old fashioned coinage as remuneration. The reason was simple, shame. Micro technology had made tracking metal coins possible but not yet cost effective. The user of old-fashioned coinage would be anonymous and safe from discovery in the virtual baby pits or the giant vagina explorer experience.

Outside it was snowing.

January 2025
<u>Cobalt, PENNSYLVANIA</u>

<u>OBITUARY</u>
January 31, 2025

Mr. Brian Scancarello, 62. Mr. Scancarello died sometime last summer and unfortunately was not found until last week. He had no known relatives in the area. Mr. Scancarello was employed for thirty years as a meta-virtual maintenance man for the Billy Jack Apartment Complex. There will be no service.

Boy Scancarello was devastated the day he saw on his iScreen (TM) that his idol and role model George O'Dowd had died from a Glittermint (TM) overdose. He had known from the Cerebral Gossip Feeds (TM) that Boy George had gotten heavily into Glittermint (TM) a deadly and vicious new designer drug that was all the rage in Business Show.

A Glittermint (TM) overdose was not a pretty thing, as it usually resulted in the unfortunate victim sneezing out his disintegrating brains through his nose and ears. Why would anyone risk such a nasty and painful death? The effect of Glittermint (TM) was said to be comparable to riding a ten hour, supersonic hundred foot wave of warm blood while feasting on chocolate boobs and ejaculating electric rainbows.

Never the less, Boy Scancarello was shattered to his core. He had spent a lifetime, since the tender age of nineteen when he saw his first Culture Club video on MTV, striving to emulate his gender bending idol. Boy Scancarello had always been unsure of his own sexual preferences, preferring not to draw any lines in the sand. He would cross them all, as George did, proudly and openly. Or not. In truth, Boy Scancarello was almost sixty years old and he was still a virgin.

But that was just a dirty technicality.

He had many other hobbies, such as building model spaceships, coin collecting (he specialized in state Quarters) and tropical fish. His fish were his passion, thick bug-eyed bottom dwellers that stared with bared sharp little pointy teeth. They were from China, *Channa argus*, but Boy Scancarello already decided that he didn't like them half as much as the piranhas his mother used to raise.

 Most of his paycheck went for things like make up, hair extensions, fish food and model glue. He was unashamed in his fashion choices, which mimicked as best as he could, Boy George's look circa 1983.

He did draw puzzled and amused looks in his everyday life as janitor at the Billy Jack Apartment Complex, a five-hundred-unit cinderblock cube that housed over three thousand people. Clanking through the complex hallways, jingling with keys and necklaces, Boy Scancarello was like a cat with a bell. Boy Scancarello with his corn rows and caftans, his heavy eye makeup and his expanding beer belly, made for a colorful sight pushing his broom down the hallways, dancing and crooning behind it. He was known also for issuing the occasional waspish witticism when he found no other way to deal with the attitudes of the troglodytes that lived there. Usually, it was teenage death poppers who harassed him. "Hey fag! Got any retro cigarettes?"

It was a summer Sunday when Boy Scancarello woke up from a beautiful dream about flying over pink trees when he plugged his iVision (TM) into his skull jack and learned the terrible news. Boy George had been at a high-altitude nightclub and had started sneezing. First there was the blood, then the seizures, then the chucks of curly brain matter, bright pink and yellow. There were pictures of it everywhere on most of the internets; some of them in 4-D.

No one will ever know what happened in Boy Scancarello's lonely apartment room just off the Walmart megadumspters that summer. No one seemed to have noticed that he didn't come to work anymore. Whether it was a heart attack or stroke or maybe even something that involved foul play or something self-inflicted that is between Boy Scancarello and his maker.

When he was found, by accident, several months later by a Biotech Crew looking for illegal stashes of compost, his badly decomposed body was face down on the living room floor, his gray shrunken fists clutched at the floor. Over his head was a clear plastic trash bag. In front of him, was a broken jar of old-fashioned coins strewn about the floor. The Hazmat cleanup crew helped themselves; there were still many parts of the country that took the coins as if they were real money.

June 2032
<u>NFL, NEVADA</u>

Johnny PK began his community service in June when the weeds were blooming and the whole slate colored earth suddenly turned various hues of unnatural neon green.

When he was busted for selling fake Mars gold on the i-internets he knew there was the possibility of doing heavy zombie time. He was relieved that his Law Giver had bargained him down to physical non-virtual community service, because being a chemically induced zombie slave was not his idea of a good time.

It sucked.

Johnny PK remembered the stories about Monkey Island. It was a small manmade island in the middle of City Park, right outside the zoo. It was surrounded by a wide, deep rock walled moat and populated by a tribe of chattery spider monkeys who clambered and begged popcorn from the spindly limbs of a stunted elm tree planted by grade school children after the fallout winters of 2024-2026.

Back then, people visiting the zoo could sit on a bench and watch the spider monkeys frolic and mooch treats. Then the economy went bad and the zoo closed down. Johnny PK remembered something about the zoo animals being sold to a fancy restaurant but that was about it.

The zoo and most of City Park was now overgrown with lush neon green weeds. The park had been taken over and was now populated by tribes of Ditch People; homeless ditch dwellers who went through the park trash barrels looking for lottery tickets or refundable food. The Ditch People were usually harmless, if not overly friendly. But they had taken over the park and a new mayor had been elected largely on the promise to fix up the park and have the Ditch People relocated into the wild somewhere.

Like Texas.

So, this was how Johnny PK found himself on Monkey Island on a fine June morning pulling neon green weeds as part of his i-court ordered physical non-virtual community service. Already he was sweating. The weeds, bright glowing green and smelling like a mixture of diesel fuel and a bag of freshly cut grass, were coming out of the greasy black dirt easily. It had been raining a few days before.

Johnny PK yanked and yanked. He loved the creosote smell of the dirt as he pulled the oily, unnaturally green weeds out by the roots. Although he was loathe to admit it Johnny PK felt great working in the June morning sun, sweating. He could see that what he was doing was making a difference. Not like spray painting rocks gold and claiming they were from Mars. Real Mars gold went for a premium because it was blue. But Johnny PK never got that.

As he pulled up the weeds and overturned the earth, he began to notice that he was pulling up a large quantity of white sea shells entangled in the root balls of the weeds. At first, he didn't think much of it, but they became more and more abundant, and Johnny PK began to wonder about finding sea shells in Nevada. He looked closer and was shocked to discover that they weren't sea shells at all, but bones.
Little bones...

Scapula's and ulnas.

Femurs and patella's.
Mandibles and vertebrae's.

Skulls and teeth.

Johnny PK looked around and he could see, even on top of the ground deep in the weeds, hundreds of these little white bones. He walked over to the stunted elm tree that graced Monkey Island. The school children that planted it in 2013 had to wait for the monkey wranglers to restrain the monkeys so they could put it in the dirt. On the far side of it, facing the entrance to the old golf cart storage, was what looked like a pyramid, roughly the size of an antique mini-fridge made out of mud and bits of paper. It had various coins and tokens pressed into it, some of them looked pretty old, like from the 1990's.

As he bent looking closer Johnny PK saw more bones around the pyramid. In fact, he saw skeletons. At first, he thought they were children and terror seized him. But then he saw they had tails and he suddenly realized what they were.

He looked up, across the moat to a group of ditch people rifling through a trash can. They were dressed in vinyl and plastic and talked to one another in a strange mixture of Spanish and German. They did not look at or pay any attention to Johnny PK. Especially after they found a disposable lap phone and some perfectly good transistor apples in the trash.

Johnny PK sat on the ground. He felt sick with the vision in his head. In his mind he saw the spider monkeys, starving because of budget cuts, neglected by a careless zoo keeper, slowly starving while gawking tourists threw popcorn and coins at them.

Johnny looked down and saw what looked like a muddy little glove at his feet. he picked it up and saw that it was a hand. A mummified monkeys hand, curled tightly into a fist.   It was holding something. Johnny PK snapped the little fingers off one at a time. They broke like candy cigarettes, turning to dust and bone, smelling of gunpowder and chlorophyll. When he got the fingers off Johnny PK saw that the hand had held a coin. A Quarter. It was almost a hundred years old.

Johnny PK saw that the ditch people were looking at him now. He put the Quarter in his pocket. Maybe he could sell it on i-bay. Maybe he could say that it had come from Mars.

On second thought, Johnny PK threw the coin at the ditch so he could watch the Ditch People scramble and fight for it, but like always, he came up short.

July 2037
<u>Anhedonia, OHIO</u>

"Does anybody have an old-fashioned coin? A Quarter?"

The Metapsychic asked the small group sitting in a circle around her. The Metapsychic looked at them, at their faces and made her calculations. The Metacenter hummed with activity, both virtual and real. Outside the polarized reflective smart wall windows, The Metapsychic could see a mob of homeless people all waiting their turn to use the virtual toilets and sex dens.

Bryce Astik had an old Quarter that he carried with him for good luck and he held it up, not fully unable to conceal his smirk. He knew full well that this new Psychic fad was a bunch of shit but his new girlfriend Belindix was into it and their relationship was not yet strong enough to bear the weight of the reality of his true thoughts or opinions. The Metapsychic spotted Bryce but did not want to take his Quarter. She knew he was not a believer. She could sense it. But no one else had any old school money, only virtual currency fobs.

Reluctantly the Metapsychic smilingly took Bryce's Quarter. Bryce sat back and gave Belindix a quick glance. She was fixed on The Metapsychic, who rolled the coin around in her hand and closed her eyes. The Metacenter meeting room grew quiet in anticipation. She rubbed the worn coin's edges, feeling the places where the grooves had worn down. This was an old coin.

It had seen a lot.

"First off I'd like to talk to you about Clepinin, the non-scalding hair growth remover that removes all hairs in less than sixty seconds using our new patented matter disintegration technology. Clepinin, so you can be as smooth on the outside as you are on the inside."

The Metapsychic then moved her hand, and on the polarized smart window wall a jolly image of Clepinin, in the form of a cartoon spray bottle, demonstrated on a cartoon bear-ape how one pump would make all the hair on the bear-ape's body jump four feet in the air, then drift and float to the floor, leaving a grinning bald bear-ape with a self-satisfied smirk. Not unlike the smirk on Bryce's face.

The Metapsychic decided that instead of just making things up she would really try to see if she could feel anything. She decided just to say out loud whatever popped into her head. What was the difference?

"I see pug dogs...sunlight...I hear woodpeckers...The Beatles..."

Bryce smirked. Belindix saw it and nudged him. He flushed with guilt and shame.

"I see...people afraid...jumping...rivers of fish...darkness and fire...dust and guitars... the beginning and the end of the world. And monkeys."

The Metapsychic suddenly handed Bryce back his Quarter. He noticed that it felt warm, almost hot in his hand and that it seemed to vibrate, but that could also be from the room erupting in applause. The Metapsychic smiled beatifically but inwardly she was disturbed. She accepted their praise and their credit fibers and nodded her approval at her audience's absolute need to believe.

March 2038
<u>Taco Bell ARKANSAS</u>

The Quarter is dropped and lost on the way home by Lanser Talnc, a seven-year-old boy coming from the i-Dream Store after buying some more old coins for his Grandfather's birthday. He had found the Quarter he was looking for, before he lost it, from the year of his grandfather's birth. The date was barely legible, but it was enough. 1963.

It was the first spring-like day of that year.

March 2041

Cheyenne-Safeway City WYOMING

The cloud in question was a fat, fluffy cumulonimbus. It was a bright brilliant white on its cottony top with gray to black shaded undertones beneath. At the downtown Cloud Speculation Brokerage in Cheyenne-Safeway City, the cloud, which was named Cumulo2017, was being carefully monitored and tracked by crystagital micro areosensors dropped into it by midget balloon droids and logged by a remote satellite laser system.

Reeve Mangum a 51-year-old cloud broker from Laramie and Randy 334 Dallam, a thirty-nine-year-old cloud speculator from Pueblo, Colorado was in a fierce dispute over ownership of Cumulo2017, which was calculated to hold seventy thousand cubic feet of expensive and potentially valuable moisture.

 Mangum had registered the cloud some twenty-seven minutes previously; Dallum had claim on the cloud for the past thirty-nine minutes, but his sonic computer line was slower that Mangum's light speed system so his regispatent was not logged in time.

The two men argued about the legalities of cloud real estate and the credibility of satellite time stamps in the Lavalounge of the Cheyenne Hologram Hawaii Hotel. Their cyber law teams brandished e-tracts signed and verified by brainscanner to be legally and morally binding.

Meanwhile Cumulo2017 gradually drifted east, where it unfortunately began to disintegrate. Flashes of spring lightning illuminated its gray edges. The fluffiness was going down, the white was not so bright now, but the color of five-year-old underwear. This devalued the cloud to the point where desperation set in.

Finally, with the consent of the cyber law teams and the holojudge on iTV, Randy 334 Dallum and Reeve Mangum agreed to an old solution to a modern problem. Reeve's cloud wrangler foreman Tommy Kissel produced his lucky Quarter. It was hardly a coin anymore. Over a third of its silver had been worn off over the years, scattered across the county in tiny atoms, scuttling back into the sweet dark earth from which it came. The smooth disc that Tommy Kissel handed the men was hardly recognizable at all. It felt smooth and thin.

 Dallum and Mangum nodded in silent agreement. Kissel flipped the blackened, tarnished coin into the air.

"Heayds." Said Dallum, never taking his eyes off the coin.

By then though it was too late. Cumulo2017 had broken up was now known as Cumulo2017a, Culumlo2017b, Culumlo2017c, Culumlo2017d, Culumlo201754897, and Culumlo20179846edg. As broken cumulofragments their value was now much lower than it had been only minutes before. The moisture thCumulo2017 carried was now vaporized back into the atmosphere instead of being transformed into biocredits in some cloud speculator's moisture metaccount.

The Quarter hit the videofloor of the Lavalounge at the Hologram Hawaii Hotel in the heart of downtown Cheyenne-Safeway City.

It spun and wobbled. The men peered at it but wondered if it was too worn and smooth to really tell which was which anymore.

September 2045
P3451,KANSAS

Tatatatatatat.

 Springtime perfume from the wind.

A bird singing in a voice he was hearing for the first time.

Tatatatatatat. A faint and far away answer.

A woman's dress rustling.

Just the hint of a distant fire.

221

August 2049
Mulkey, OKLAHOMA

Pulsing, pulsing.

The wet earthen smell of benzene and heat.

Green shimmers.

Flashes of cool lightning.

Sleep.

May 2053
<u>Penzoil River, OKLAHOMA</u>

"Ding"

"What'd you find son?"

(Disappointed)

"Just an old coin. Looks like a Quarter."

"From what year?"

"I can't tell. It's too worn. Looks like silver though and not composite."

"Well, unless you want to keep it, we have no use for it."

"No, I can't use the silver. "

(Pause. Throws Quarter into the river.)

"Look at that. Those fucking fish are everywhere."

Summer 2063
<u>Thule County, OKLAHOMA</u>

Thousands of the black shiny slimy snakehead fish snuffled and croaked like frogs all through the day and the night. Their thrashing and gasping had become part of the soundscape, and their sudden ubiquitousness was taken for granted over the past few decades. People adapted as they always do, dodging their snapping grunting heads as they savaged their way about their days. An explosion of trendy snakehead fish restaurants opened, as their flesh was very tasty, but the sheer volume of their numbers soon overwhelmed even the most dedicated snakehead harvesters, and when the novelty wore off no one much felt like eating them anymore.

Dubbed "Frankenfish" by the media because of their determined, aggressive nature and sharp plentiful teeth, the snakeheads originated in China. They had been dumped into US rivers and lakes by people who had bought them for food and evidently changed their minds... Once the story got around in the early 1990's some people with their own reasons began deliberately introducing the bug-eyed predators into delicate ecosystems which they soon overwhelmed.

The snakehead fish had steadily overflowed from rivers and lakes after being introduced into the waterways as far back as the 1970's. Some said it was carelessness, others a hideous conspiracy.

The sudden population explosion and rapid extinction of lesser species of fish was unexpected and shocking and the voracious predators ate their way from Maryland to Oklahoma in seventy short years.

Capable of living for a period of time out of the water and prone to dragging itself along with its leg-like flippers, the snakehead fish had earned a sinister reputation. Stories of snakehead attacks were legion in the first flush of panic. They flopped around on lakeshores chasing children and killing dogs.

Stories of them coming up through toilets and loping onto lawns, while semi true, were not quite as apocalyptic as they were presented in the press. That would all come later.

While the snakehead fish was an angry hunter, it was also largely indifferent to anything other than its immediate prey. Though they were killed by the tens of thousands, they reproduced fast thanks to the ever-present supply of food in every path they took. Now there were so many of them that even manmade municipal ponds and park lakes were full of the snorting, snapping predators, who lashed about in the crowded water, transforming it into a massive squirming mega cell.

By the hot summer of 2063, National Homeland Security Guard units were called in from the former Middle East to detail kill the infestations. Mass sonic burnings, laser routing and chemical flashing were used on the hordes but too little effect. While snakehead fish by the score died in towns and municipalities, those in the wild lakes and rivers thrived. Citizens organized "threshing" expeditions where entire communities would come out with stunners, sonic weapons, light guns, football bats, i-golf clubs, laser machetes and other, even more crude weapons to club and beat the squirming, jaw snapping, ever advancing fish.

They became larger and more aggressive as they moved west. They found it easier somehow to withstand the crushing pressure out of water and their rudimentary lungs began to grow stronger through a sudden burst of evolution that not even the smartest of all the scientists in the world could understand or explain. Their fins became strong supporting their huge fat bodies on the land. If anyone had been paying close attention, they would have noticed that a snakehead fish out of water in 1997 was very different to the snakehead fish out of water in 2032.

In Michigan alone seven people had been killed by snakehead attacks including one small boy, Gary Neselrode, who fell into a pond full of the fish and was skeletonized in seconds. In Elmira, New York, a state of emergency was declared by Governor Kyle Hogg when hundreds of snakehead fish hopped and flopped their way from a brick pond into downtown and stopped traffic for over ten hours. The cleanup alone cost the state over two hundred and seventy trillion dollars. It all happened so suddenly and so irrevocably that most people chose to adapt rather than fight it. Playgrounds were rusted and empty of children and a booming business for "Indoor Recreation Arenas" enabled its inventor Mark Tat, to purchase his own country and turn it into the most expensive desert resort in the world located in central Australia. All desert land suddenly became premium real estate with Utah and Arizona suddenly becoming the "new Aspen."

****

It is dusk and the air hangs heavy with humidity as a herd of snakeheads leaves the river, dragging their big bellies across the hard scratchy ground. Voraciously, they devour everything in their path, garbage, plants, cans, dogs, anything at all.

The largest of them, at over four feet in length, is on point, like a general, twisting its blinkless eyes back and forth in search for food. The hungry herd of Frankenfish continues forward, snuffling and eating, fulfilling a destiny so ancient it hardly seems real at all. The sky breaks open and the rain starts to come. The snakehead

fish can breathe easier now and their skin is smoothed and soothed by the return of their element.
A perfectly wafer shaped black disk catches one's attention in the mud and reflexively the fish uses its massive tooth lined lower jaw to scoop at the ground, clawing up and consuming the badly worn and tarnished silver disk without a second thought.

It is an old coin, a 1963D Quarter dollar, one of 135,288,184 minted that year.